WEEDED

Gary's Garden

BY GARY NORTHFIELD

David Fickling Books
the PHOENIX

SCHOLASTIC

FOR BEN

Thank you for leading
me up the right garden path.

Thanks to Lisa Murphy for helping color the cover.

First published in the United Kingdom in 2014 as *Gary's Garden: Book 1* by David Fickling Books, 31 Beaumont Street, Oxford OX1 2NP. *www.davidficklingbooks.com*

Library of Congress Control Number: 2015942071

ISBN 978-0-545-86183-0

10 9 8 7 6 5 4 3 2 1 16 17 18 19 20

Printed in the U.S.A.
First edition, July 2016

CONTENTS

 this way for all the fun, pals!

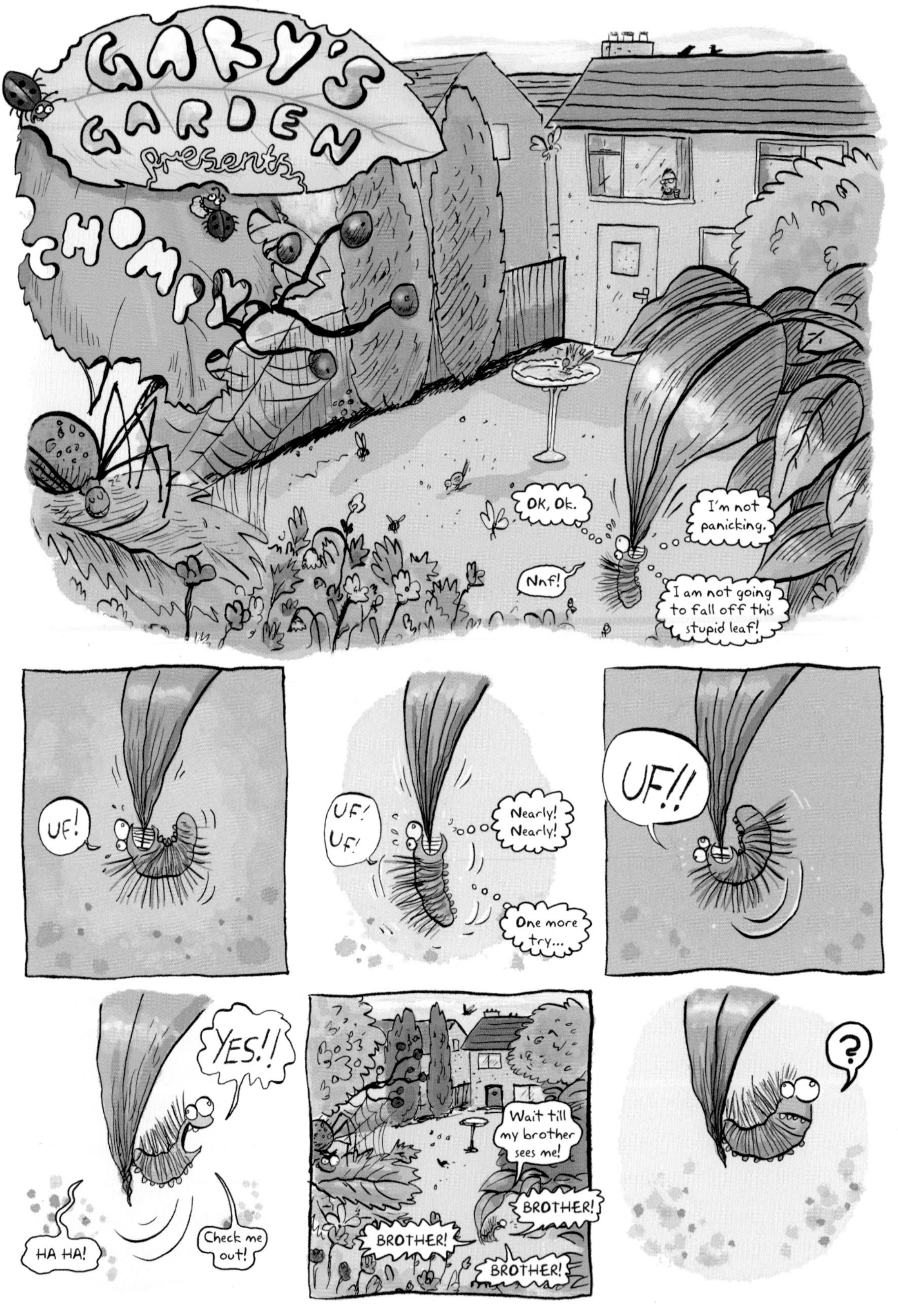
GARY'S GARDEN
presents
CHOMPY
OK, Ok.
I'm not panicking.
Nnf!
I am not going to fall off this stupid leaf!
UF!
UF! UF!
Nearly! Nearly!
One more try...
UF!!
YES!!
HA HA!
Check me out!
Wait till my brother sees me!
BROTHER!
BROTHER!
BROTHER!
?

BROTHER! BROTHER! BROTHER!

Yes, yes. I'm here. What is it?

Look, brother! I'm standing on the end of a leaf! I'm a daredevil!

Bah. I don't have time for this.

Try not to fall off and kill yourself. We're having dinner soon.

Ha! Falling off is for losers!

I'm a DAREDEVIL!

Hello?

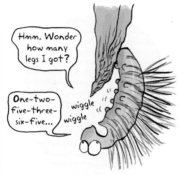

Hmm. Wonder how many legs I got?

One-two-five-three-six-five...

wiggle wiggle

Oop.

PLATCH!

Ahem.

Hello. I am caterpillar.

Me too!

Gasp!

NO! YOU NOT caterpillar!!

JUMP!

You WORM!

But we both wiggles, right?

We're the same!

NO!!

NOT THE SAME !!!!

5

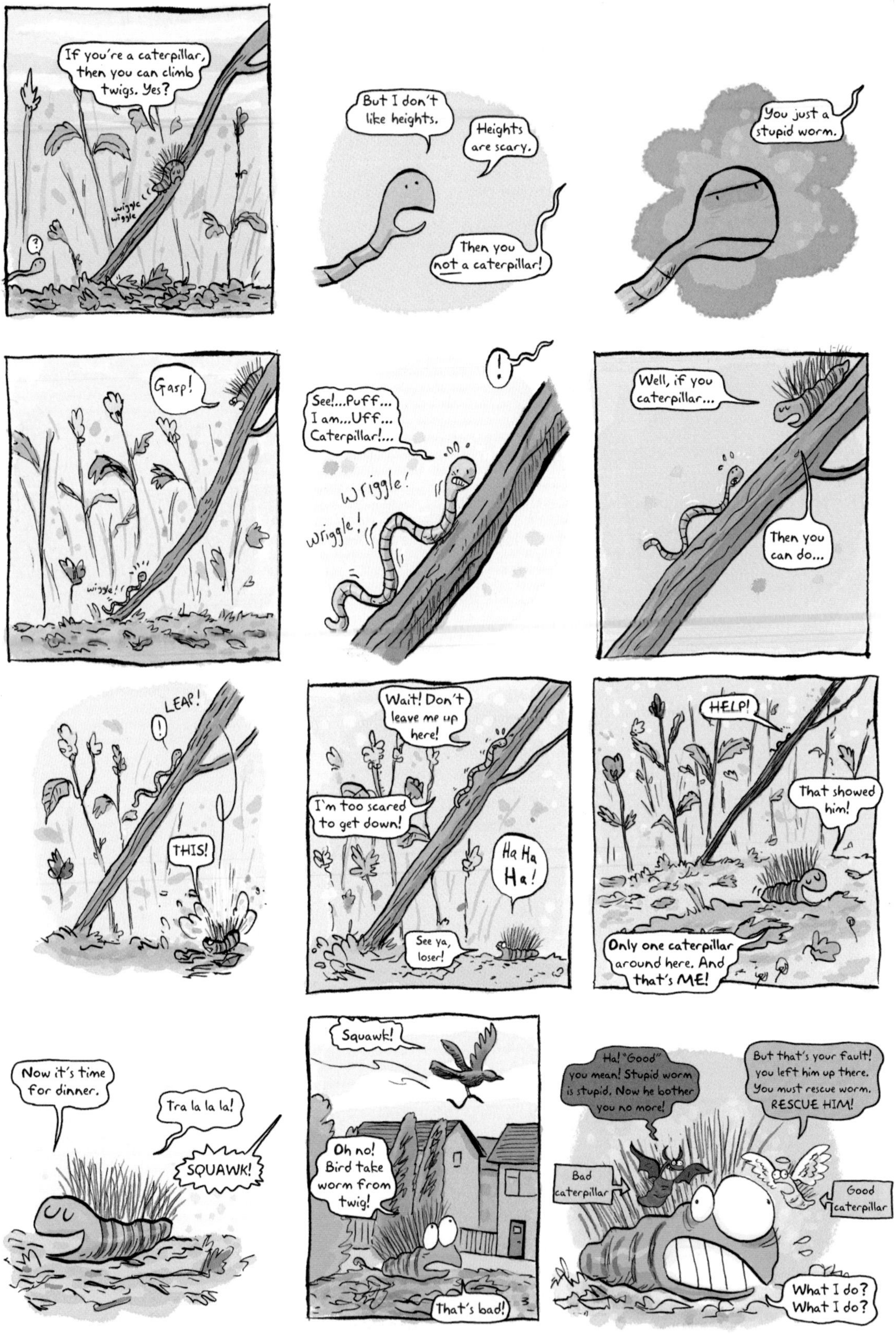

If you're a caterpillar, then you can climb twigs. Yes?
?
wiggle wiggle
But I don't like heights.
Heights are scary.
Then you not a caterpillar!
You just a stupid worm.
Gasp!
wiggle!!
!
See!...Puff... I am...Uff... Caterpillar!...
Wriggle!
Wriggle!
Well, if you caterpillar...
Then you can do...
LEAP!
!
THIS!
Wait! Don't leave me up here!
I'm too scared to get down!
Ha Ha Ha!
See ya, loser!
HELP!
That showed him!
Only one caterpillar around here. And that's ME!
Now it's time for dinner.
Tra la la la!
SQUAWK!
Squawk!
Oh no! Bird take worm from twig!
That's bad!
Ha! "Good" you mean! Stupid worm is stupid. Now he bother you no more!
But that's your fault! You left him up there. You must rescue worm. RESCUE HIM!
Bad caterpillar
Good caterpillar
What I do? What I do?

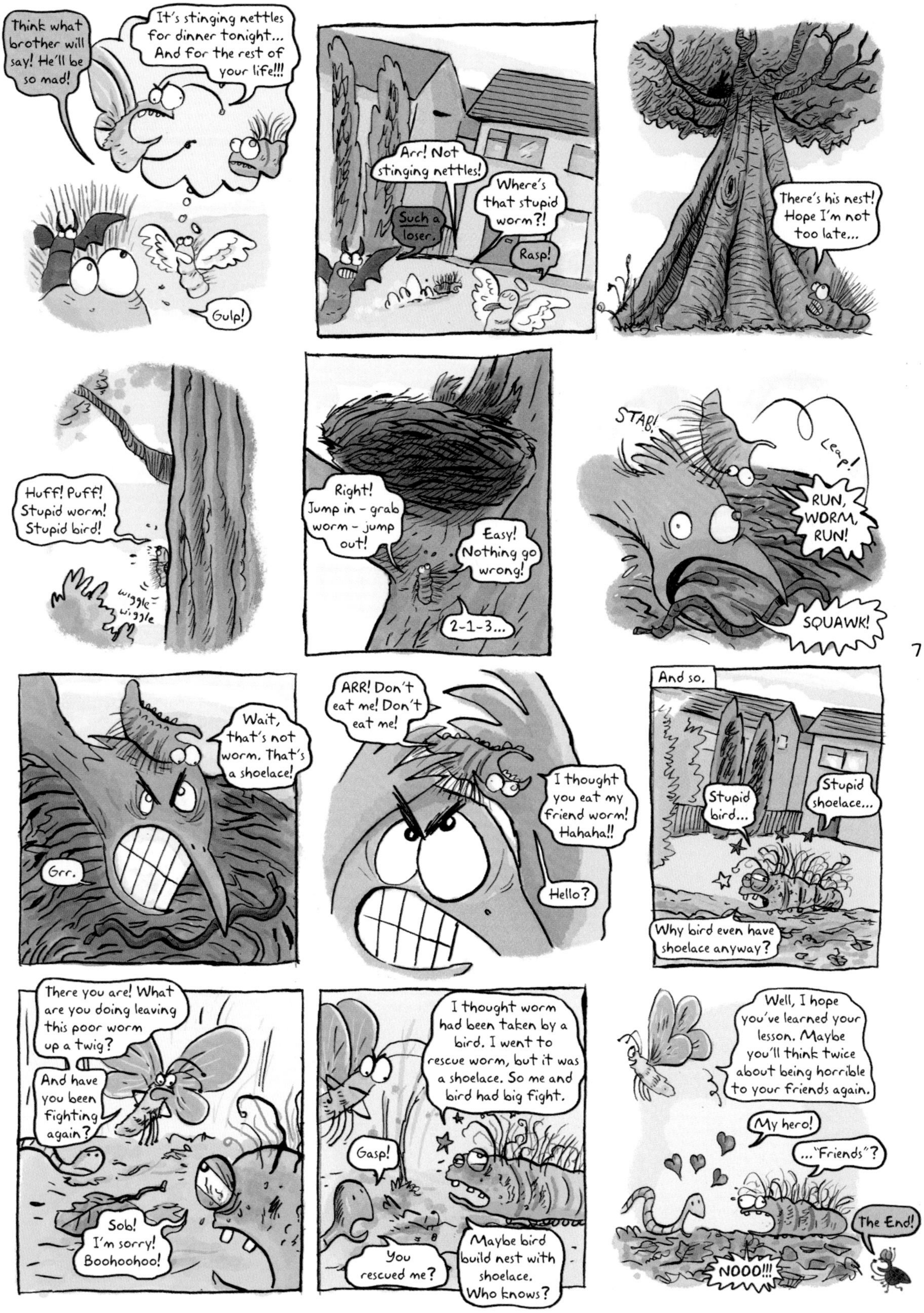
Think what brother will say! He'll be so mad!
It's stinging nettles for dinner tonight... And for the rest of your life!!!
Gulp!
Arr! Not stinging nettles!
Such a loser.
Where's that stupid worm?!
Rasp!
There's his nest! Hope I'm not too late...
Huff! Puff! Stupid worm! Stupid bird!
wiggle wiggle
Right! Jump in - grab worm - jump out!
Easy! Nothing go wrong!
2-1-3...
STAB!
Leap!
RUN, WORM, RUN!
SQUAWK!
Wait, that's not worm. That's a shoelace!
Grr.
ARR! Don't eat me! Don't eat me!
I thought you eat my friend worm! Hahaha!!
Hello?
And so.
Stupid bird...
Stupid shoelace...
Why bird even have shoelace anyway?
There you are! What are you doing leaving this poor worm up a twig?
And have you been fighting again?
Sob! I'm sorry! Boohoohoo!
I thought worm had been taken by a bird. I went to rescue worm, but it was a shoelace. So me and bird had big fight.
Gasp!
You rescued me?
Maybe bird build nest with shoelace. Who knows?
Well, I hope you've learned your lesson. Maybe you'll think twice about being horrible to your friends again.
My hero!
..."Friends"?
The End!
NOOO!!!

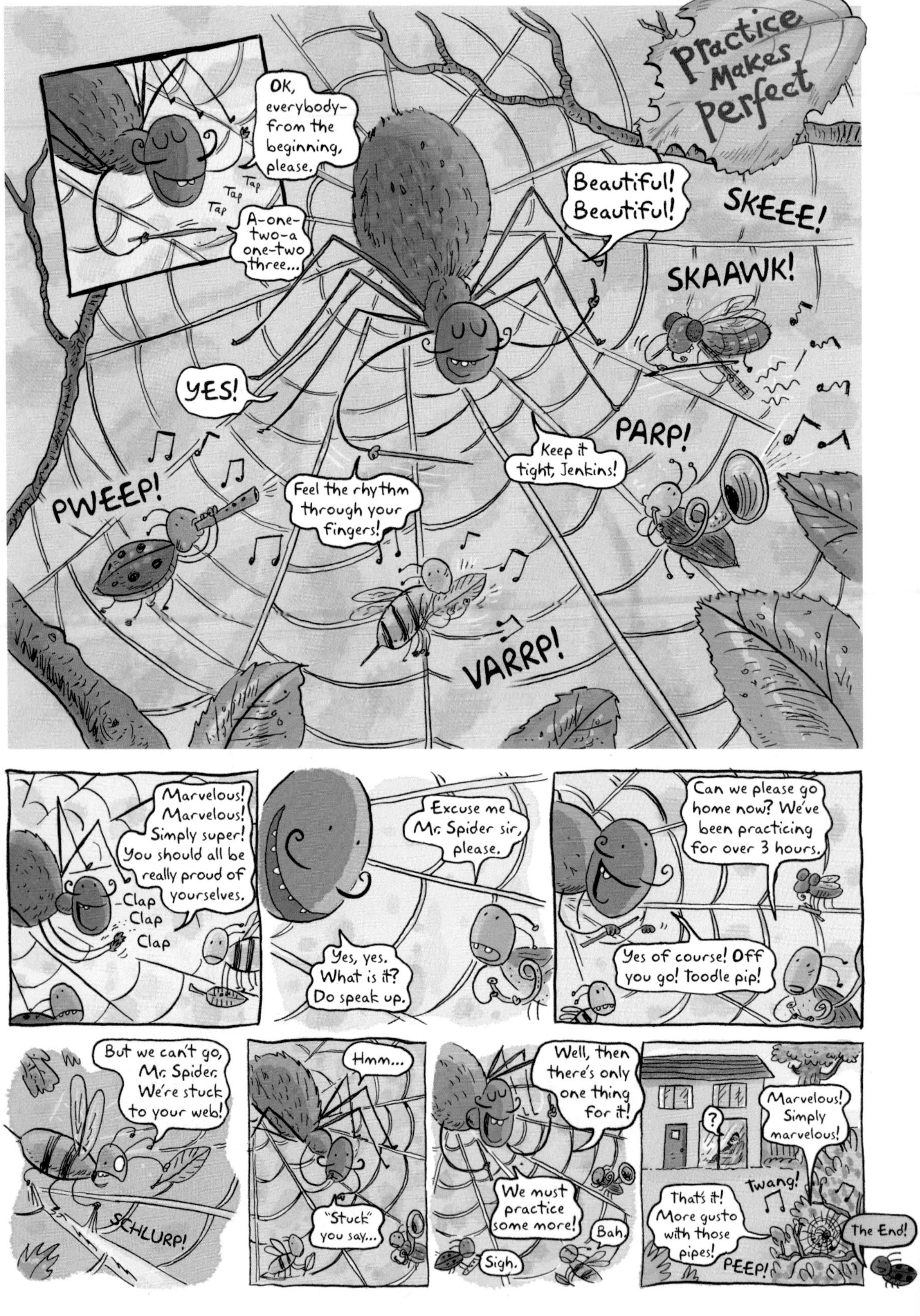
Practice Makes Perfect
OK, everybody-from the beginning, please.
Tap Tap Tap
A-one-two-a one-two three...
Beautiful! Beautiful!
SKEEE!
SKAAWK!
YES!
PARP!
Keep it tight, Jenkins!
PWEEP!
Feel the rhythm through your fingers!
VARRP!
Marvelous! Marvelous! Simply super! You should all be really proud of yourselves.
Clap Clap Clap
Excuse me Mr. Spider sir, please.
Yes, yes. What is it? Do speak up.
Can we please go home now? We've been practicing for over 3 hours.
Yes of course! Off you go! Toodle pip!
But we can't go, Mr. Spider. We're stuck to your web!
SCHLURP!
Hmm...
"Stuck" you say...
Well, then there's only one thing for it!
We must practice some more!
Bah.
Sigh.
?
Marvelous! Simply marvelous!
Twang!
That's it! More gusto with those pipes!
PEEP!
The End!

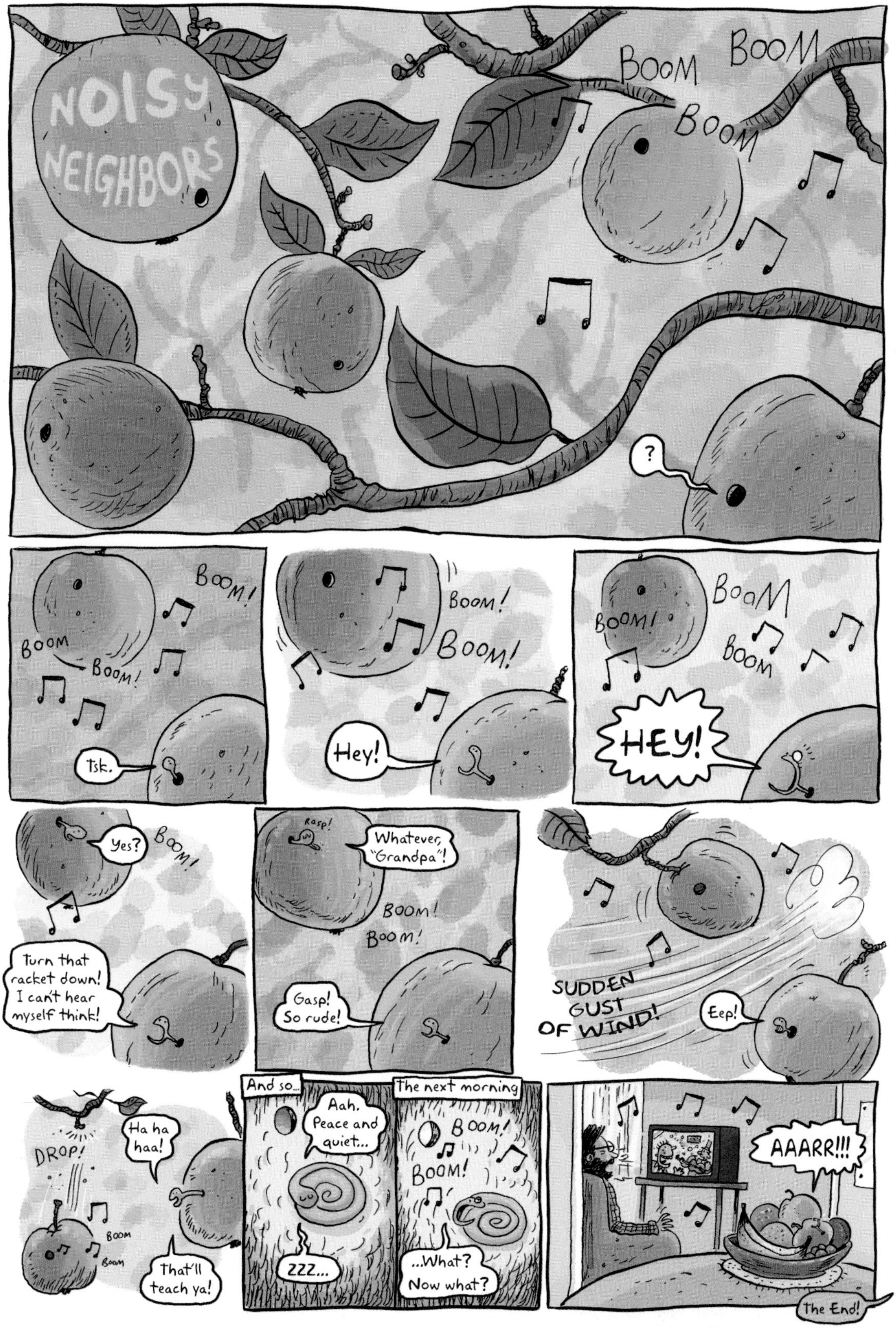
NOISY NEIGHBORS
BOOM BOOM
BOOM
?
BOOM!
BOOM
BOOM!
Tsk.
BOOM!
BOOM!
Hey!
BOOM
BOOM!
BOOM
HEY!
Yes?
BOOM!
Turn that racket down! I can't hear myself think!
Rasp!
Whatever, "Grandpa"!
BOOM!
BOOM!
Gasp! So rude!
SUDDEN GUST OF WIND!
Eep!
DROP!
Ha ha haa!
BOOM
Boom
That'll teach ya!
And so...
Aah. Peace and quiet...
ZZZ...
The next morning
BOOM!
BOOM!
...What? Now what?
AAARR!!!
The End!

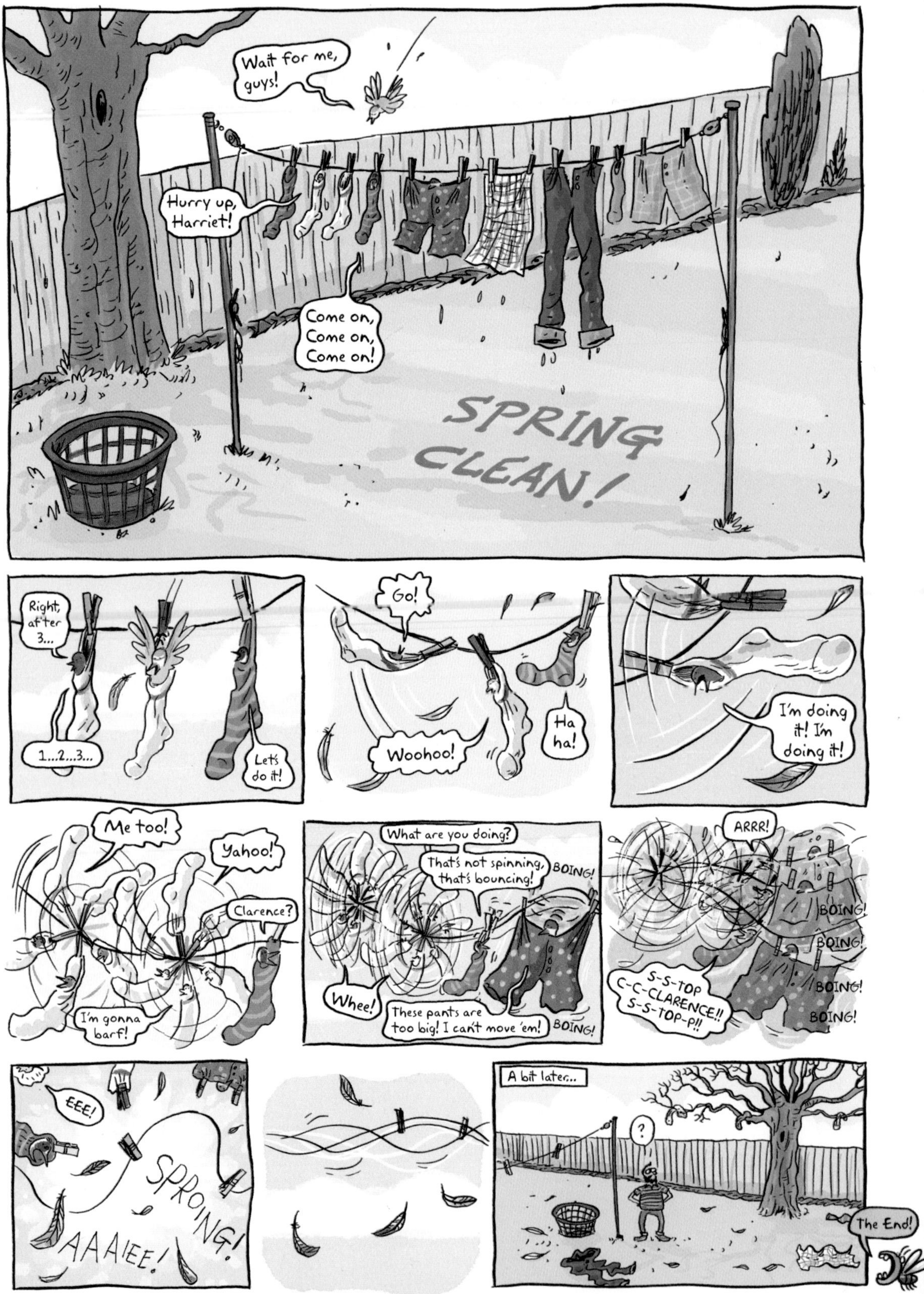
Wait for me, guys!
Hurry up, Harriet!
Come on, Come on, Come on!
SPRING CLEAN!
Right, after 3...
1...2...3...
Let's do it!
Go!
Woohoo!
Ha ha!
I'm doing it! I'm doing it!
Me too!
Yahoo!
Clarence?
I'm gonna barf!
What are you doing?
That's not spinning, that's bouncing!
BOING!
Whee!
These pants are too big! I can't move 'em!
BOING!
ARRR!
BOING!
BOING!
BOING!
BOING!
S-S-TOP C-C-CLARENCE!! S-S-TOP-P!!
EEE!
SPROING!
AAAIEE!
A bit later...
?
The End!

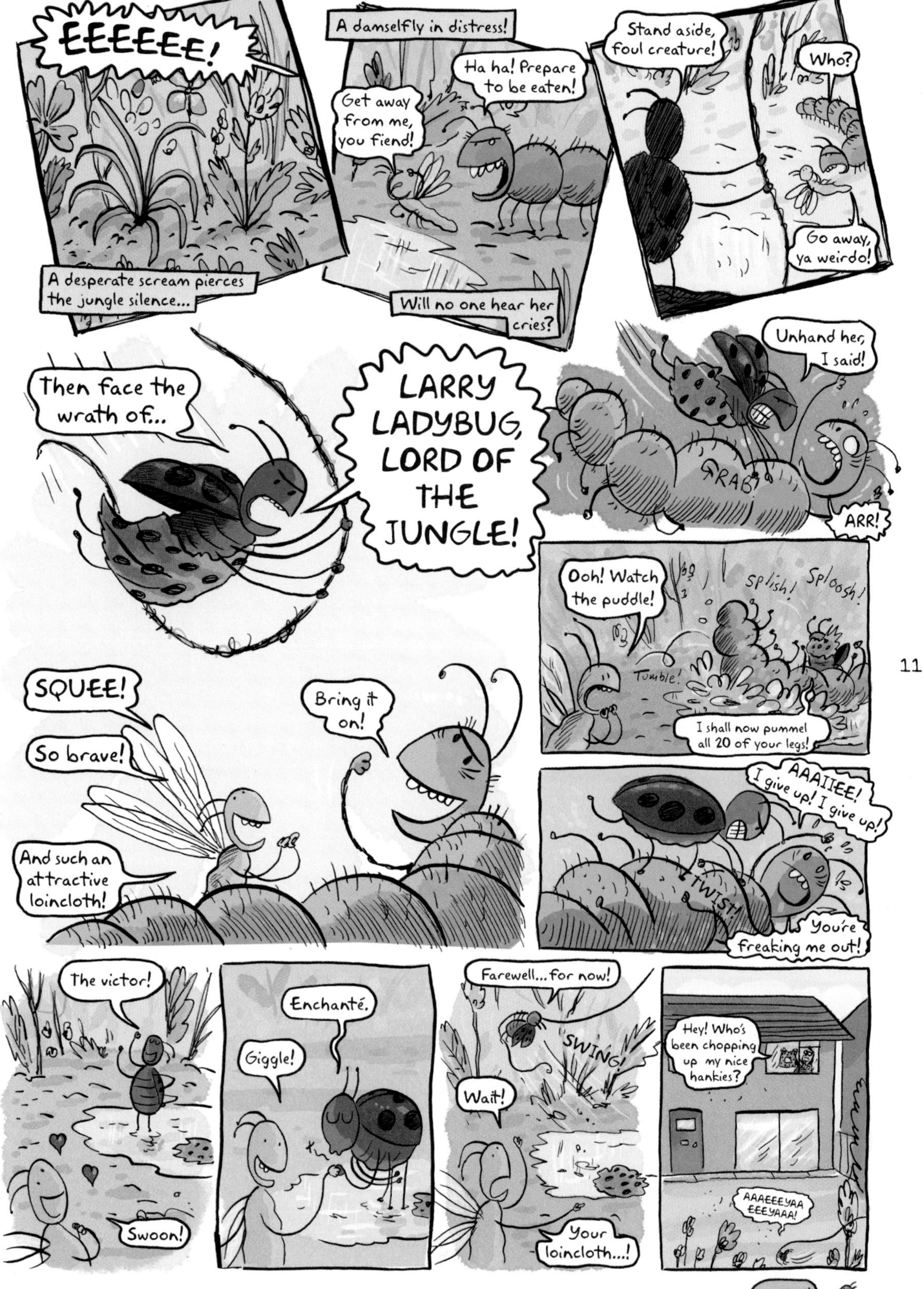
EEEEEE!
A desperate scream pierces the jungle silence...
A damselfly in distress!
Get away from me, you fiend!
Ha ha! Prepare to be eaten!
Will no one hear her cries?
Stand aside, foul creature!
Who?
Go away, ya weirdo!
Then face the wrath of...
LARRY LADYBUG, LORD OF THE JUNGLE!
Unhand her, I said!
GRAB!
ARR!
Ooh! Watch the puddle!
Splish! Sploosh!
Tumble!
I shall now pummel all 20 of your legs!
SQUEE!
So brave!
And such an attractive loincloth!
Bring it on!
AAAIIEE! I give up! I give up!
TWIST!
You're freaking me out!
The victor!
Swoon!
Enchanté.
Giggle!
Farewell... for now!
SWING!
Wait!
Your loincloth...!
Hey! Who's been chopping up my nice hankies?
AAAEEEYAA EEEYAAA!
The End!

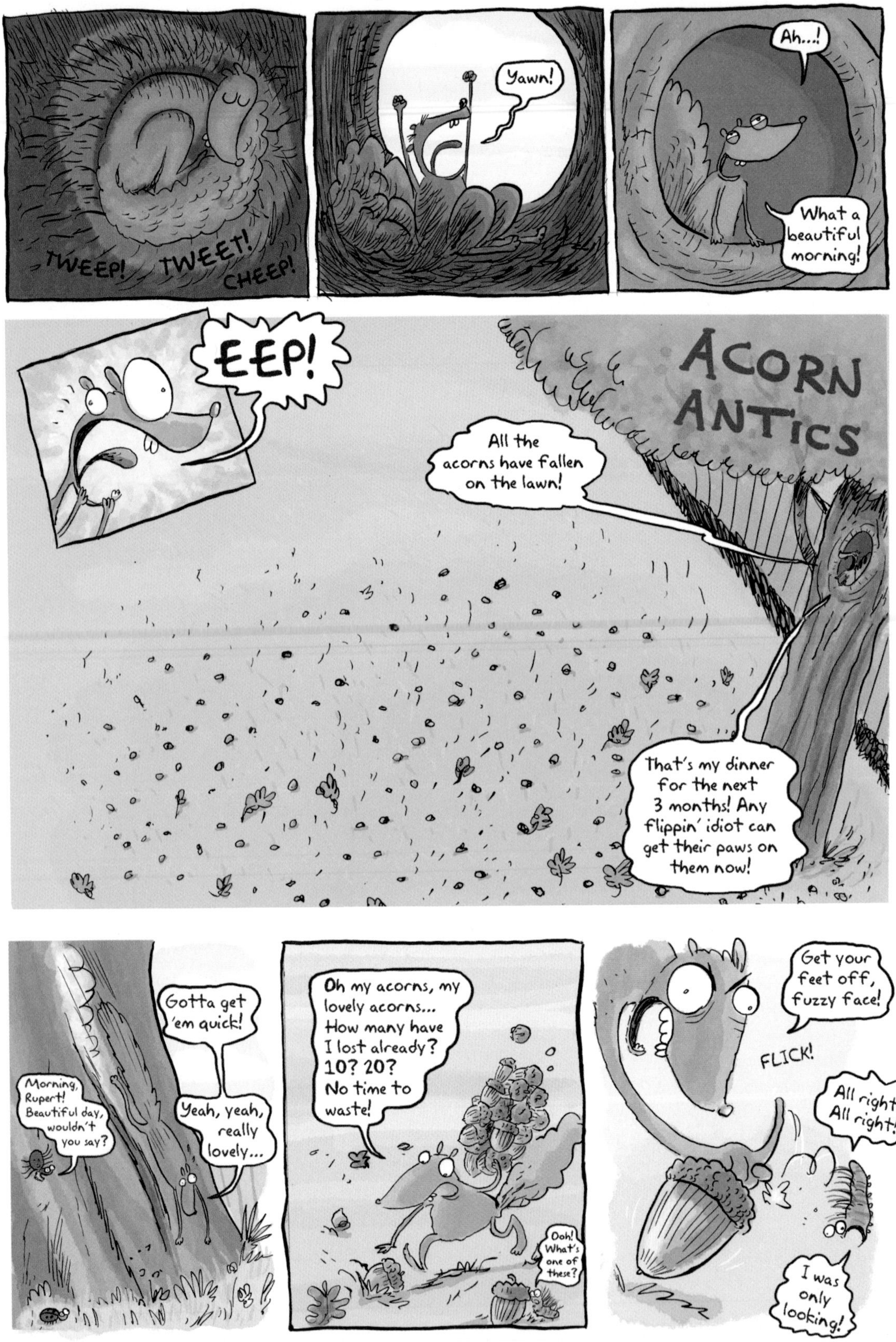
TWEEP! TWEET! CHEEP!
Yawn!
Ah...!
What a beautiful morning!
EEP!
ACORN ANTICS
All the acorns have fallen on the lawn!
That's my dinner for the next 3 months! Any flippin' idiot can get their paws on them now!
Morning, Rupert! Beautiful day, wouldn't you say?
Gotta get 'em quick!
Yeah, yeah, really lovely...
Oh my acorns, my lovely acorns... How many have I lost already? 10? 20? No time to waste!
Ooh! What's one of these?
Get your feet off, fuzzy face!
FLICK!
All right! All right!
I was only looking!

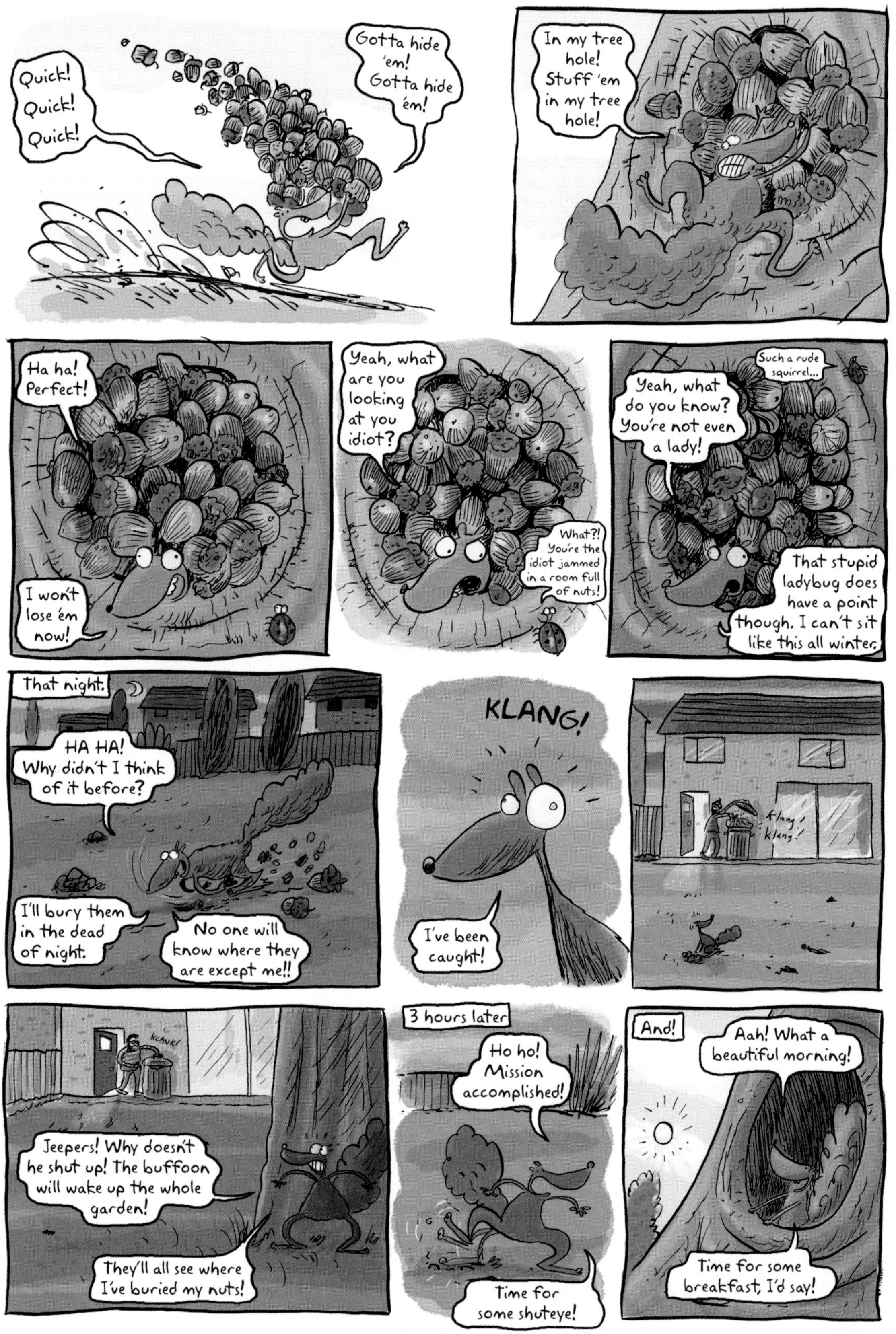

Quick! Quick! Quick!
Gotta hide 'em! Gotta hide 'em!
In my tree hole! Stuff 'em in my tree hole!
Ha ha! Perfect!
I won't lose 'em now!
Yeah, what are you looking at you idiot?
What?! You're the idiot jammed in a room full of nuts!
Such a rude squirrel...
Yeah, what do you know? You're not even a lady!
That stupid ladybug does have a point though. I can't sit like this all winter.
That night.
HA HA! Why didn't I think of it before?
I'll bury them in the dead of night.
No one will know where they are except me!!
KLANG!
I've been caught!
Klang! Klang!
KLANK!
Jeepers! Why doesn't he shut up! The buffoon will wake up the whole garden!
They'll all see where I've buried my nuts!
3 hours later
Ho ho! Mission accomplished!
Time for some shuteye!
And!
Aah! What a beautiful morning!
Time for some breakfast, I'd say!

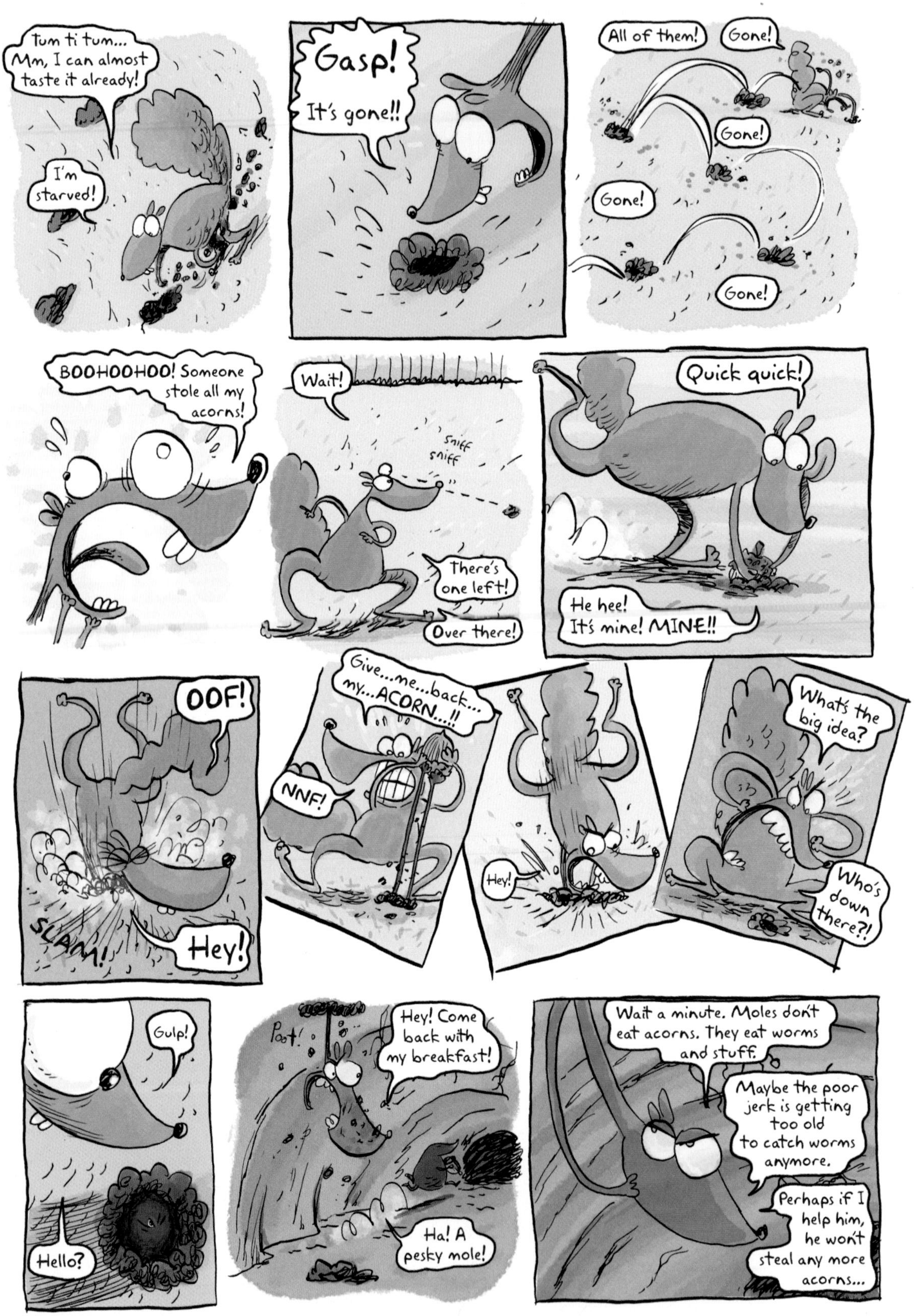
Tum ti tum... Mm, I can almost taste it already!
I'm starved!
Gasp!
It's gone!!
All of them!
Gone!
Gone!
Gone!
Gone!
BOOHOOHOO! Someone stole all my acorns!
Wait!
sniff sniff
There's one left!
Over there!
Quick quick!
He hee! It's mine! MINE!!
OOF!
SLAM!
Hey!
Give...me...back... my...ACORN...!!
NNF!
Hey!
What's the big idea?
Who's down there?!
Gulp!
Hello?
Poot!
Hey! Come back with my breakfast!
Ha! A pesky mole!
Wait a minute. Moles don't eat acorns. They eat worms and stuff.
Maybe the poor jerk is getting too old to catch worms anymore.
Perhaps if I help him, he won't steal any more acorns...

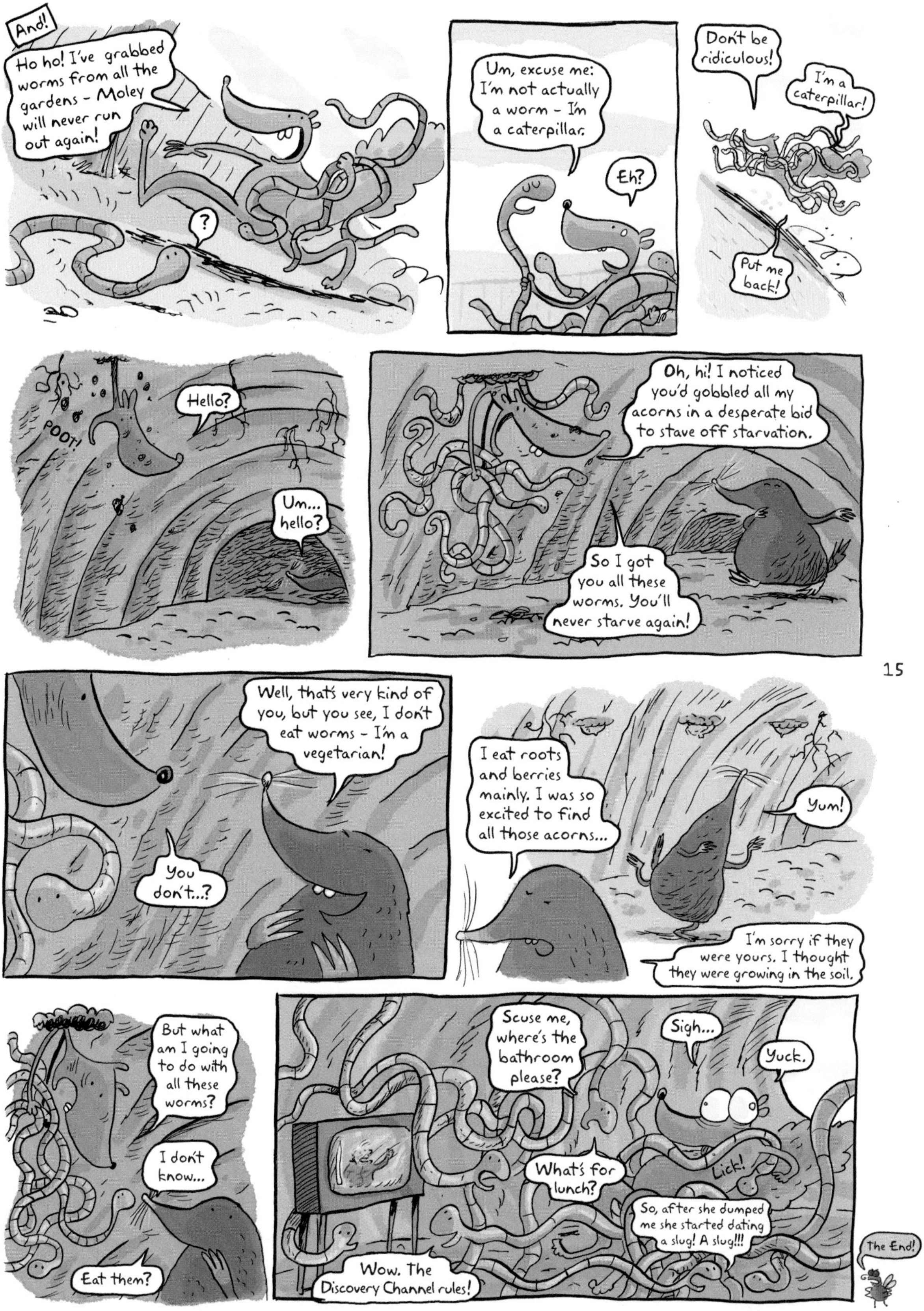

And!
Ho ho! I've grabbed worms from all the gardens - Moley will never run out again!
?
Um, excuse me: I'm not actually a worm - I'm a caterpillar.
Eh?
Don't be ridiculous!
I'm a caterpillar!
Put me back!
POOT!
Hello?
Um... hello?
Oh, hi! I noticed you'd gobbled all my acorns in a desperate bid to stave off starvation.
So I got you all these worms. You'll never starve again!
Well, that's very kind of you, but you see, I don't eat worms - I'm a vegetarian!
You don't...?
I eat roots and berries mainly. I was so excited to find all those acorns...
Yum!
I'm sorry if they were yours. I thought they were growing in the soil.
But what am I going to do with all these worms?
I don't know...
Eat them?
Scuse me, where's the bathroom please?
Sigh...
Yuck.
What's for lunch?
Lick!
So, after she dumped me she started dating a slug! A slug!!!
Wow. The Discovery Channel rules!
The End!

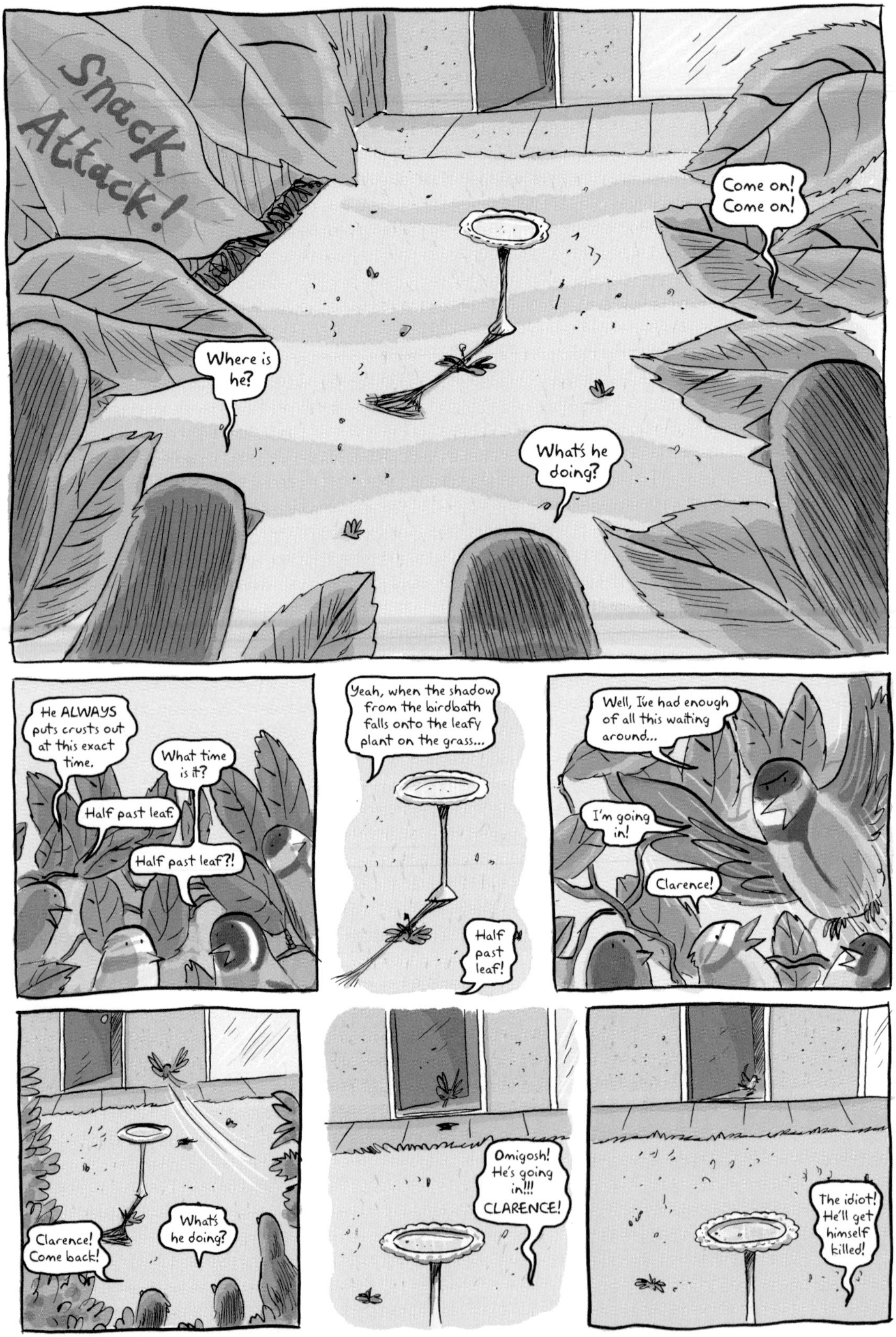
Snack Attack!
Come on! Come on!
Where is he?
What's he doing?
He ALWAYS puts crusts out at this exact time.
What time is it?
Half past leaf.
Half past leaf?!
Yeah, when the shadow from the birdbath falls onto the leafy plant on the grass...
Half past leaf!
Well, I've had enough of all this waiting around...
I'm going in!
Clarence!
Clarence! Come back!
What's he doing?
Omigosh! He's going in!!! CLARENCE!
The idiot! He'll get himself killed!

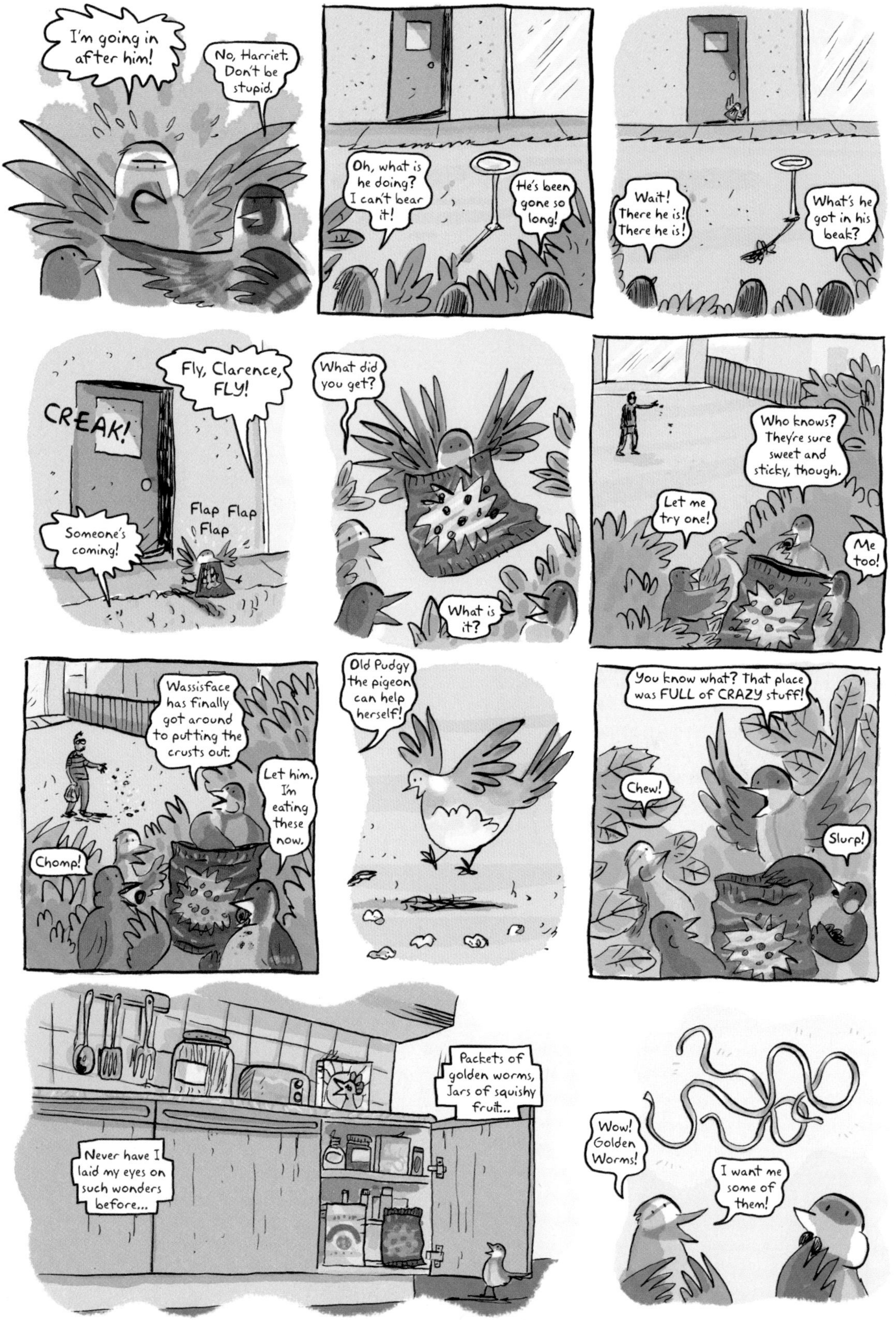
I'm going in after him!
No, Harriet. Don't be stupid.
Oh, what is he doing? I can't bear it!
He's been gone so long!
Wait! There he is! There he is!
What's he got in his beak?
Fly, Clarence, FLY!
CREAK!
Someone's coming!
Flap Flap Flap
What did you get?
What is it?
Who knows? They're sure sweet and sticky, though.
Let me try one!
Me too!
Wassisface has finally got around to putting the crusts out.
Let him. I'm eating these now.
Chomp!
Old Pudgy the pigeon can help herself!
You know what? That place was FULL of CRAZY stuff!
Chew!
Slurp!
Never have I laid my eyes on such wonders before...
Packets of golden worms, Jars of squishy fruit...
Wow! Golden Worms!
I want me some of them!

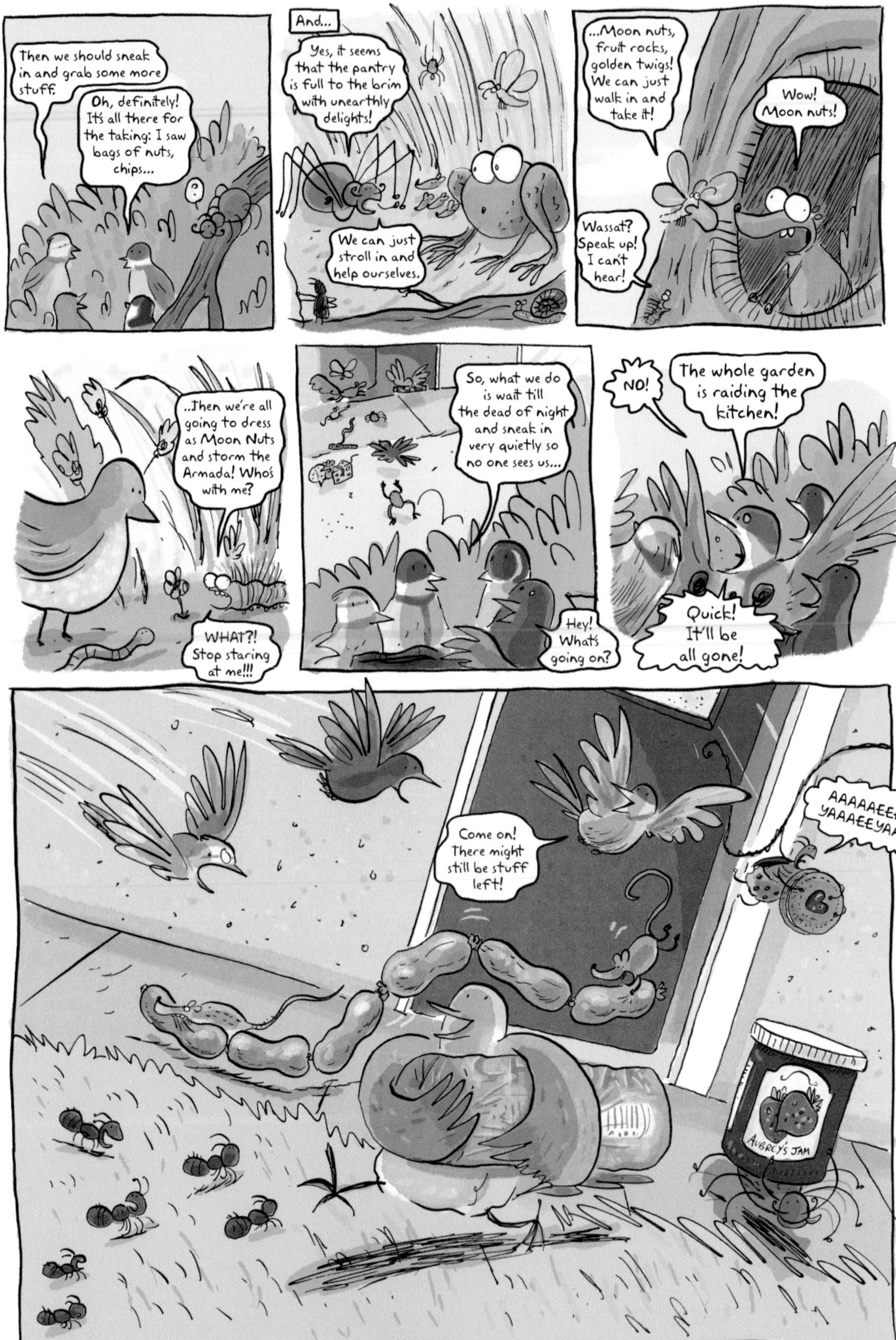
Then we should sneak in and grab some more stuff.
Oh, definitely! It's all there for the taking: I saw bags of nuts, chips...
?
And...
Yes, it seems that the pantry is full to the brim with unearthly delights!
We can just stroll in and help ourselves.
...Moon nuts, fruit rocks, golden twigs! We can just walk in and take it!
Wow! Moon nuts!
Wassat? Speak up! I can't hear!
..Then we're all going to dress as Moon Nuts and storm the Armada! Who's with me?
WHAT?! Stop staring at me!!!
So, what we do is wait till the dead of night and sneak in very quietly so no one sees us...
Hey! What's going on?
NO!
The whole garden is raiding the kitchen!
Quick! It'll be all gone!
Come on! There might still be stuff left!
AAAAAEEE YAAAEEYAA!
AUBREY'S JAM

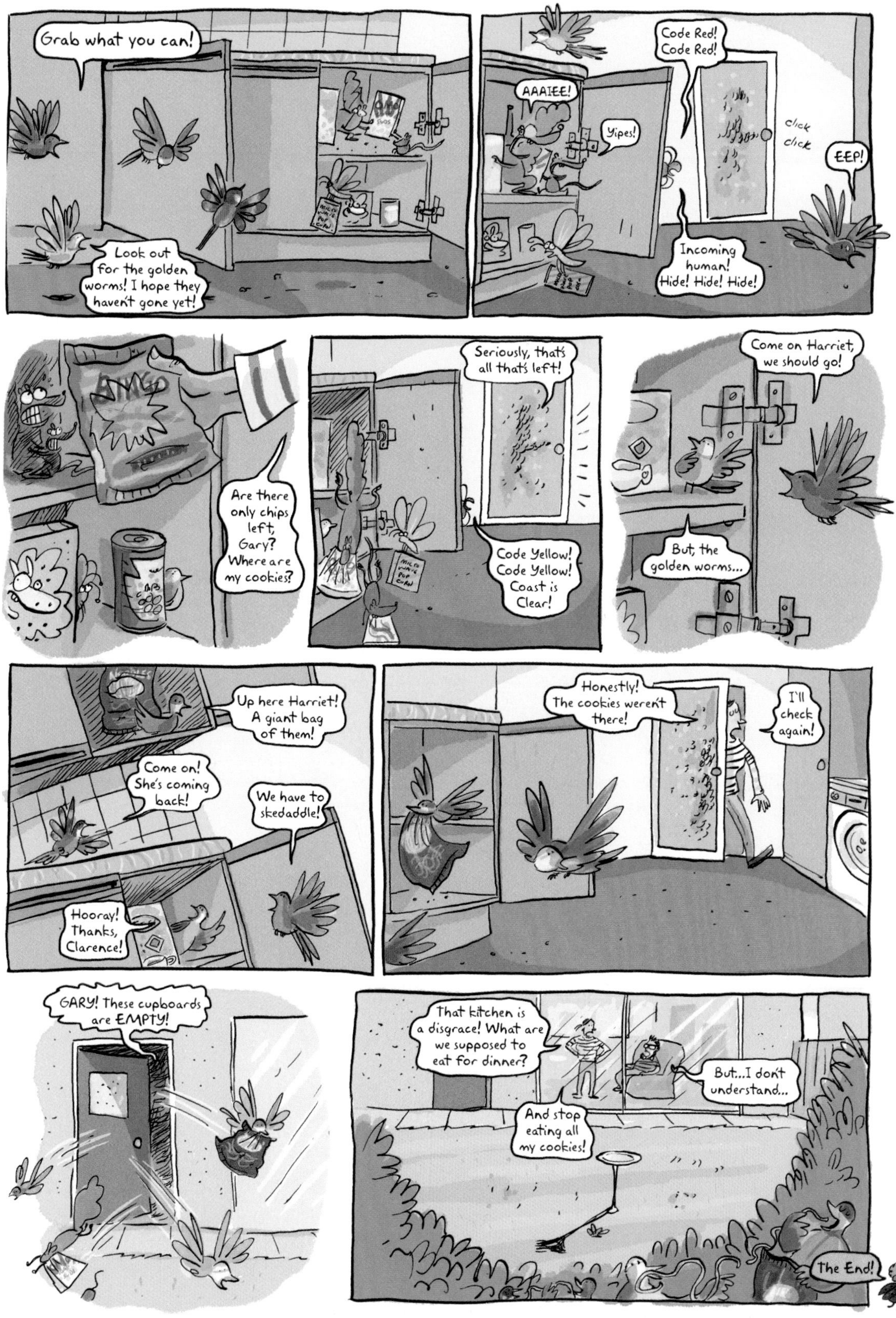
Grab what you can!
Look out for the golden worms! I hope they haven't gone yet!
Code Red! Code Red!
AAAIEE!
Yipes!
click click
EEP!
Incoming human! Hide! Hide! Hide!
Are there only chips left, Gary? Where are my cookies?
Seriously, that's all that's left!
Code Yellow! Code Yellow! Coast is Clear!
Come on Harriet, we should go!
But, the golden worms...
Up here Harriet! A giant bag of them!
Come on! She's coming back!
We have to skedaddle!
Hooray! Thanks, Clarence!
Honestly! The cookies weren't there!
I'll check again!
GARY! These cupboards are EMPTY!
That kitchen is a disgrace! What are we supposed to eat for dinner?
But...I don't understand...
And stop eating all my cookies!
The End!

First Legs
Sigh...

?
SPROING!
!
wiggle!
wiggle!
Woohoo!
Ooh!
Gee!
Scoosh!
Wow!
RASP!
Scoosh!
Gasp!
So rude!
Hahaha!
Yay!
tut!
WHIZZ!
WHOOSH!
Watch it!
Zip!

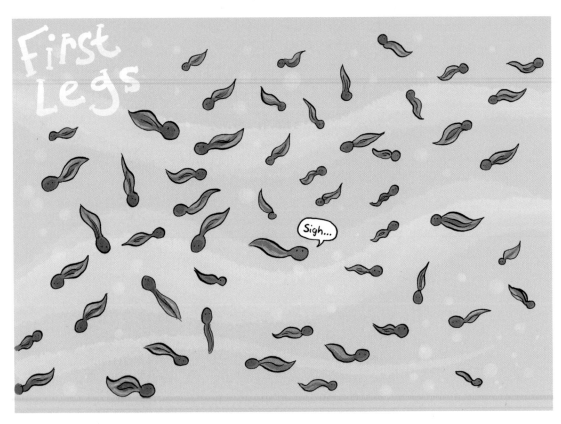

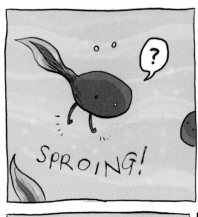

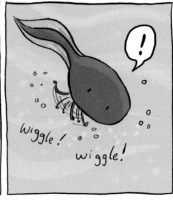

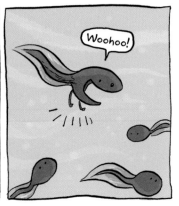

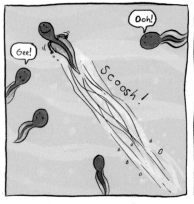

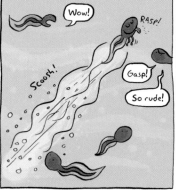

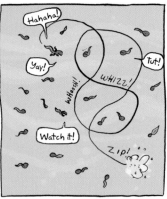

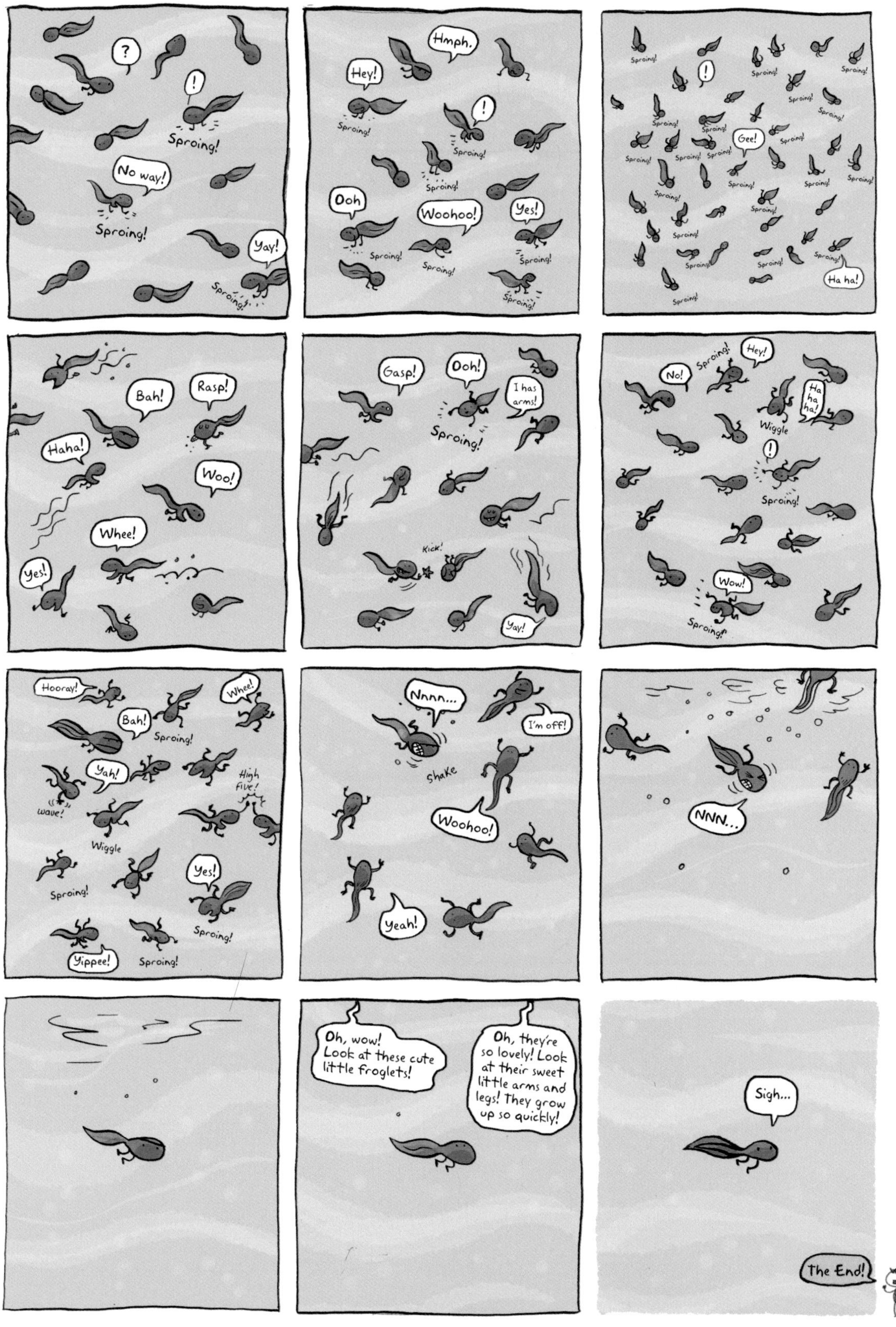
?
!
Sproing!
No way!
Sproing!
Yay!
Sproing!
Hmph.
Hey!
Sproing!
!
Sproing!
Sproing!
Ooh
Woohoo!
Yes!
Sproing!
Sproing!
Sproing!
Sproing!
Gee!
Ha ha!
Bah!
Rasp!
Haha!
Woo!
Whee!
Yes!
Gasp!
Ooh!
I has arms!
Sproing!
Kick!
Yay!
No!
Sproing!
Hey!
Ha ha ha!
Wiggle
!
Sproing!
Wow!
Sproing!
Hooray!
Whee!
Bah!
Sproing!
Yah!
High five!
Wave!
Wiggle
Yes!
Sproing!
Sproing!
Yippee!
Sproing!
Nnnn...
I'm off!
Shake
Woohoo!
Yeah!
NNN...
Oh, wow! Look at these cute little froglets!
Oh, they're so lovely! Look at their sweet little arms and legs! They grow up so quickly!
Sigh...
The End!

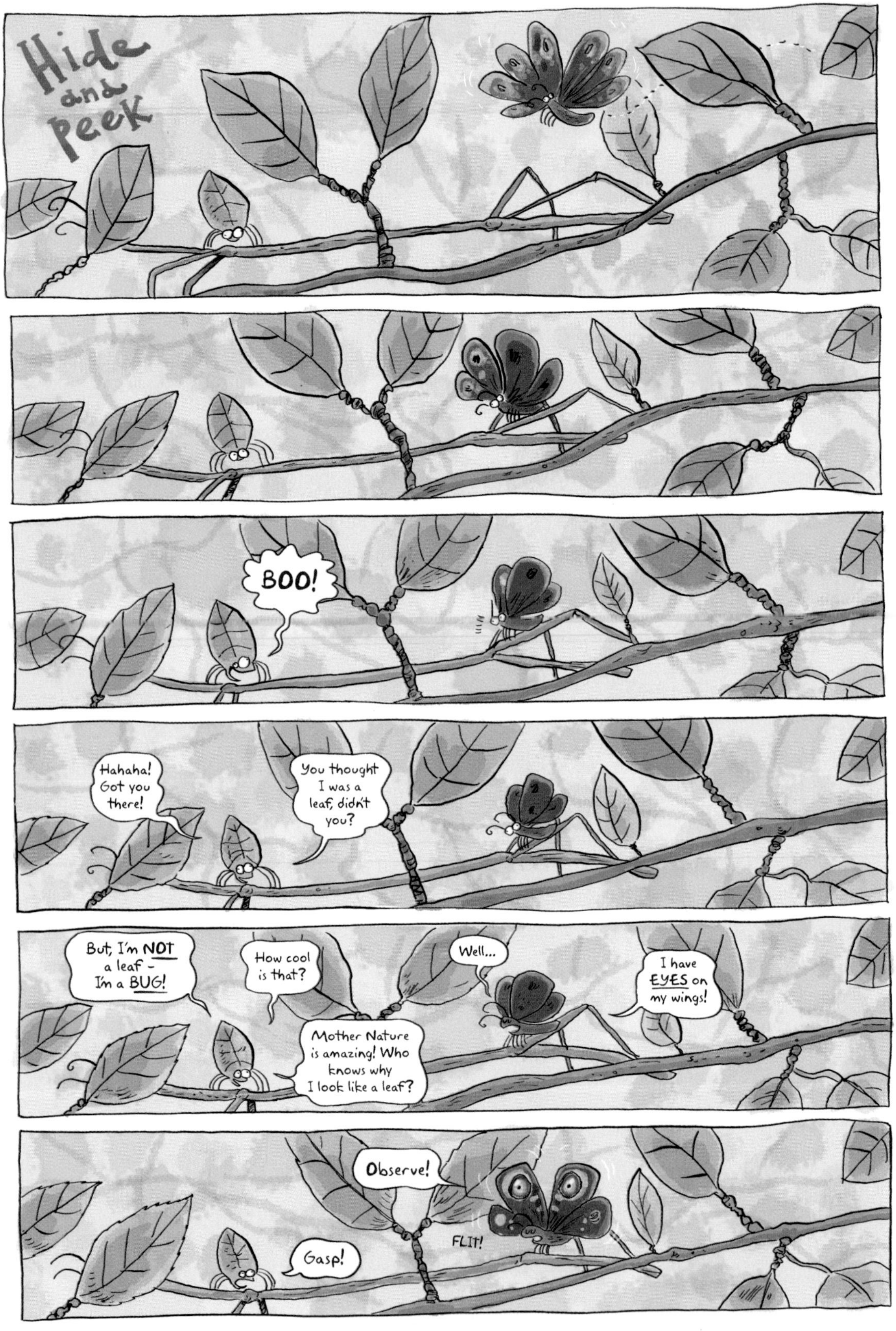

Hide and Peek
BOO!
Hahaha! Got you there!
You thought I was a leaf, didn't you?
But, I'm NOT a leaf - I'm a BUG!
How cool is that?
Mother Nature is amazing! Who knows why I look like a leaf?
Well...
I have EYES on my wings!
Observe!
FLIT!
Gasp!

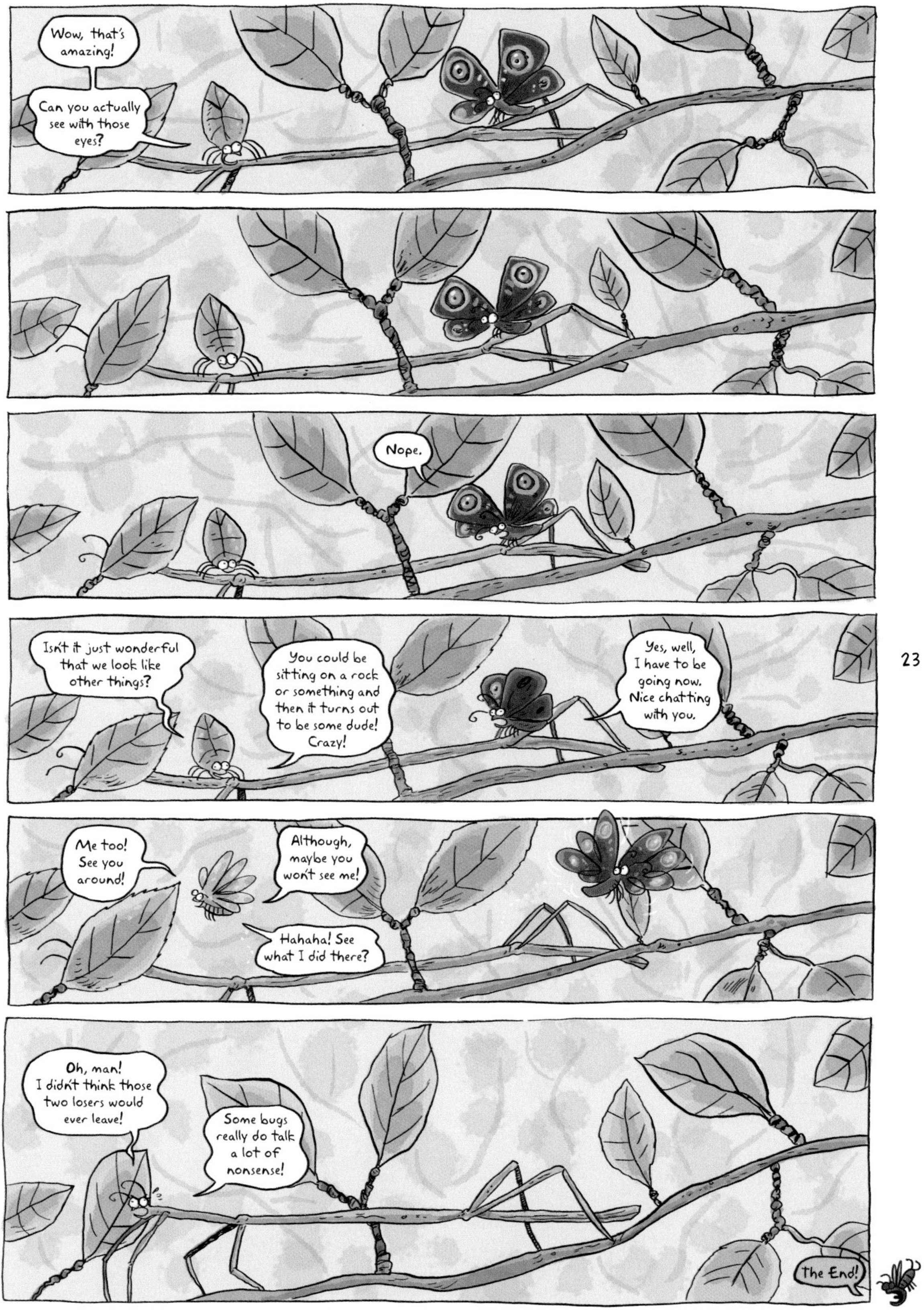
Wow, that's amazing!
Can you actually see with those eyes?
Nope.
Isn't it just wonderful that we look like other things?
You could be sitting on a rock or something and then it turns out to be some dude! Crazy!
Yes, well, I have to be going now. Nice chatting with you.
Me too! See you around!
Although, maybe you won't see me!
Hahaha! See what I did there?
Oh, man! I didn't think those two losers would ever leave!
Some bugs really do talk a lot of nonsense!
The End!

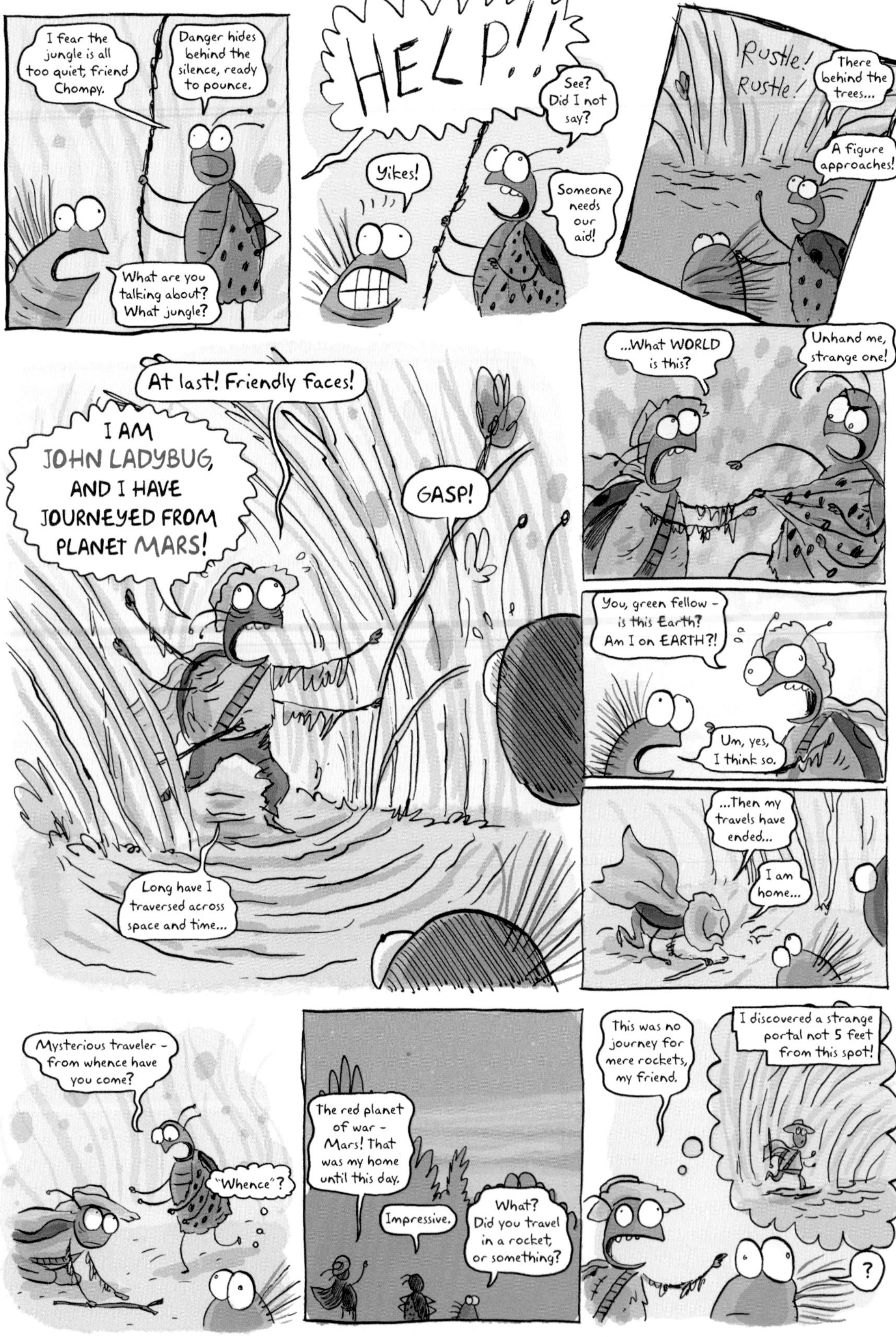

I fear the jungle is all too quiet, friend Chompy.
Danger hides behind the silence, ready to pounce.
What are you talking about? What jungle?
HELP!!
Yikes!
See? Did I not say?
Someone needs our aid!
Rustle! Rustle!
There behind the trees...
A figure approaches!
At last! Friendly faces!
I AM JOHN LADYBUG, AND I HAVE JOURNEYED FROM PLANET MARS!
GASP!
Long have I traversed across space and time...
...What WORLD is this?
Unhand me, strange one!
You, green fellow - is this Earth? Am I on EARTH?!
Um, yes, I think so.
...Then my travels have ended...
I am home...
Mysterious traveler - from whence have you come?
"Whence"?
The red planet of war - Mars! That was my home until this day.
Impressive.
What? Did you travel in a rocket, or something?
This was no journey for mere rockets, my friend.
I discovered a strange portal not 5 feet from this spot!
?

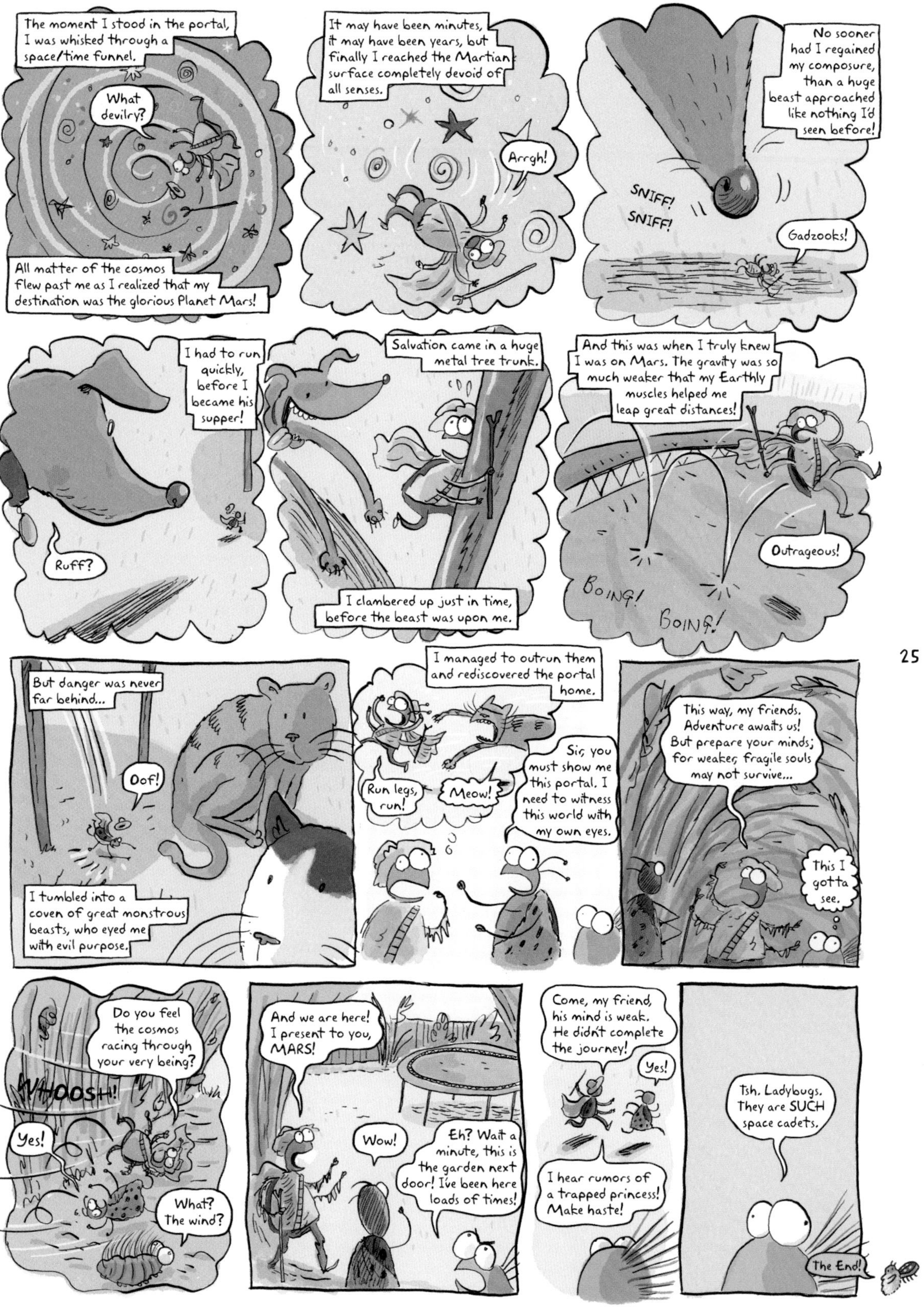
The moment I stood in the portal, I was whisked through a space/time funnel.
What devilry?
All matter of the cosmos flew past me as I realized that my destination was the glorious Planet Mars!
It may have been minutes, it may have been years, but finally I reached the Martian surface completely devoid of all senses.
Arrgh!
No sooner had I regained my composure, than a huge beast approached like nothing I'd seen before!
SNIFF! SNIFF!
Gadzooks!
I had to run quickly, before I became his supper!
Ruff?
Salvation came in a huge metal tree trunk.
I clambered up just in time, before the beast was upon me.
And this was when I truly knew I was on Mars. The gravity was so much weaker that my Earthly muscles helped me leap great distances!
Outrageous!
BOING! BOING!
But danger was never far behind...
Oof!
I tumbled into a coven of great monstrous beasts, who eyed me with evil purpose.
I managed to outrun them and rediscovered the portal home.
Run legs, run!
Meow!
Sir, you must show me this portal. I need to witness this world with my own eyes.
This way, my friends. Adventure awaits us! But prepare your minds; for weaker, fragile souls may not survive...
This I gotta see.
Do you feel the cosmos racing through your very being?
WHOOSH!
Yes!
What? The wind?
And we are here! I present to you, MARS!
Wow!
Eh? Wait a minute, this is the garden next door! I've been here loads of times!
Come, my friend, his mind is weak. He didn't complete the journey!
Yes!
I hear rumors of a trapped princess! Make haste!
Tsh. Ladybugs. They are SUCH space cadets.
The End!

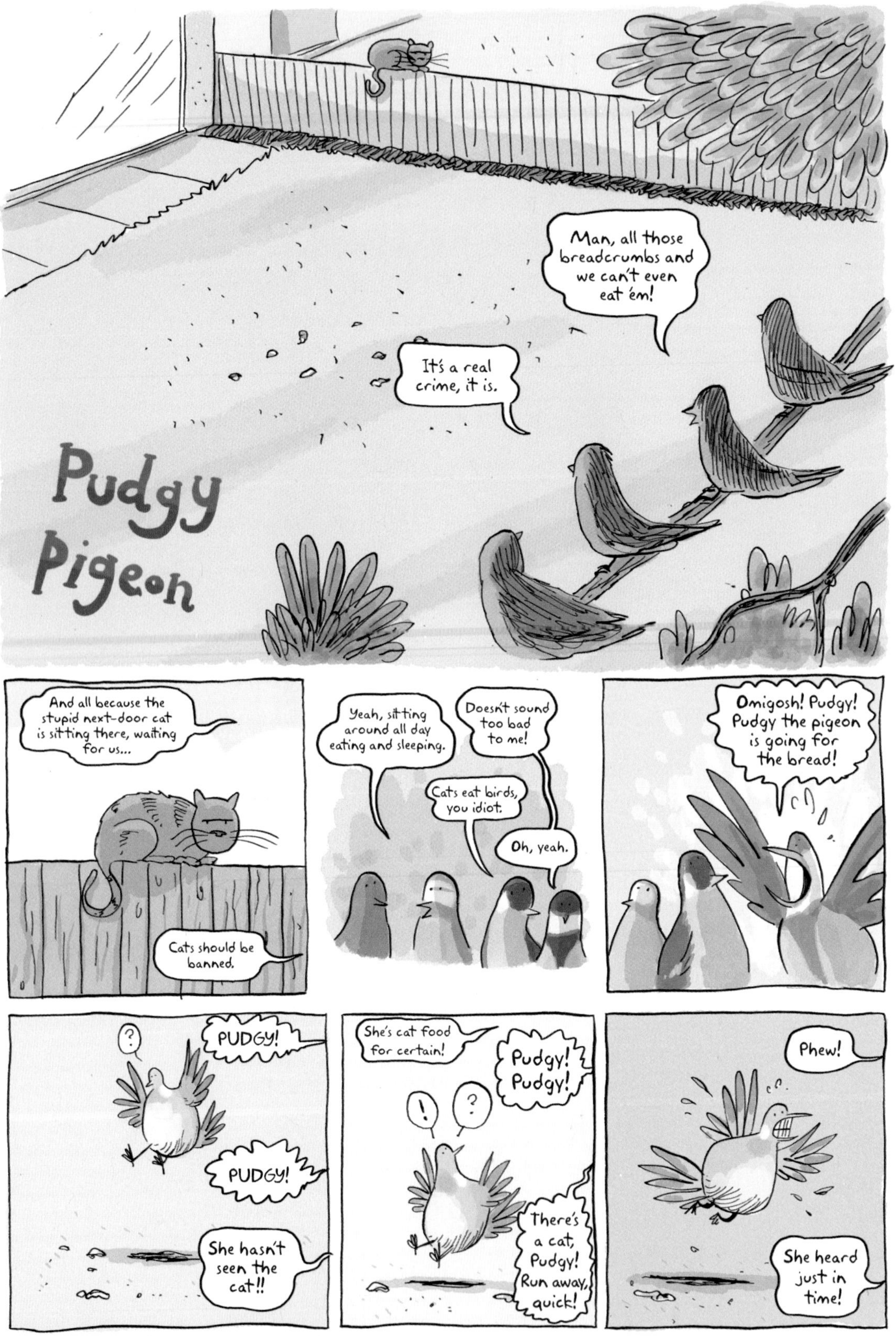
Pudgy Pigeon
Man, all those breadcrumbs and we can't even eat 'em!
It's a real crime, it is.
And all because the stupid next-door cat is sitting there, waiting for us...
Cats should be banned.
Yeah, sitting around all day eating and sleeping.
Doesn't sound too bad to me!
Cats eat birds, you idiot.
Oh, yeah.
Omigosh! Pudgy! Pudgy the pigeon is going for the bread!
?
PUDGY!
PUDGY!
She hasn't seen the cat!!
She's cat food for certain!
Pudgy! Pudgy!
!
?
There's a cat, Pudgy! Run away, quick!
Phew!
She heard just in time!

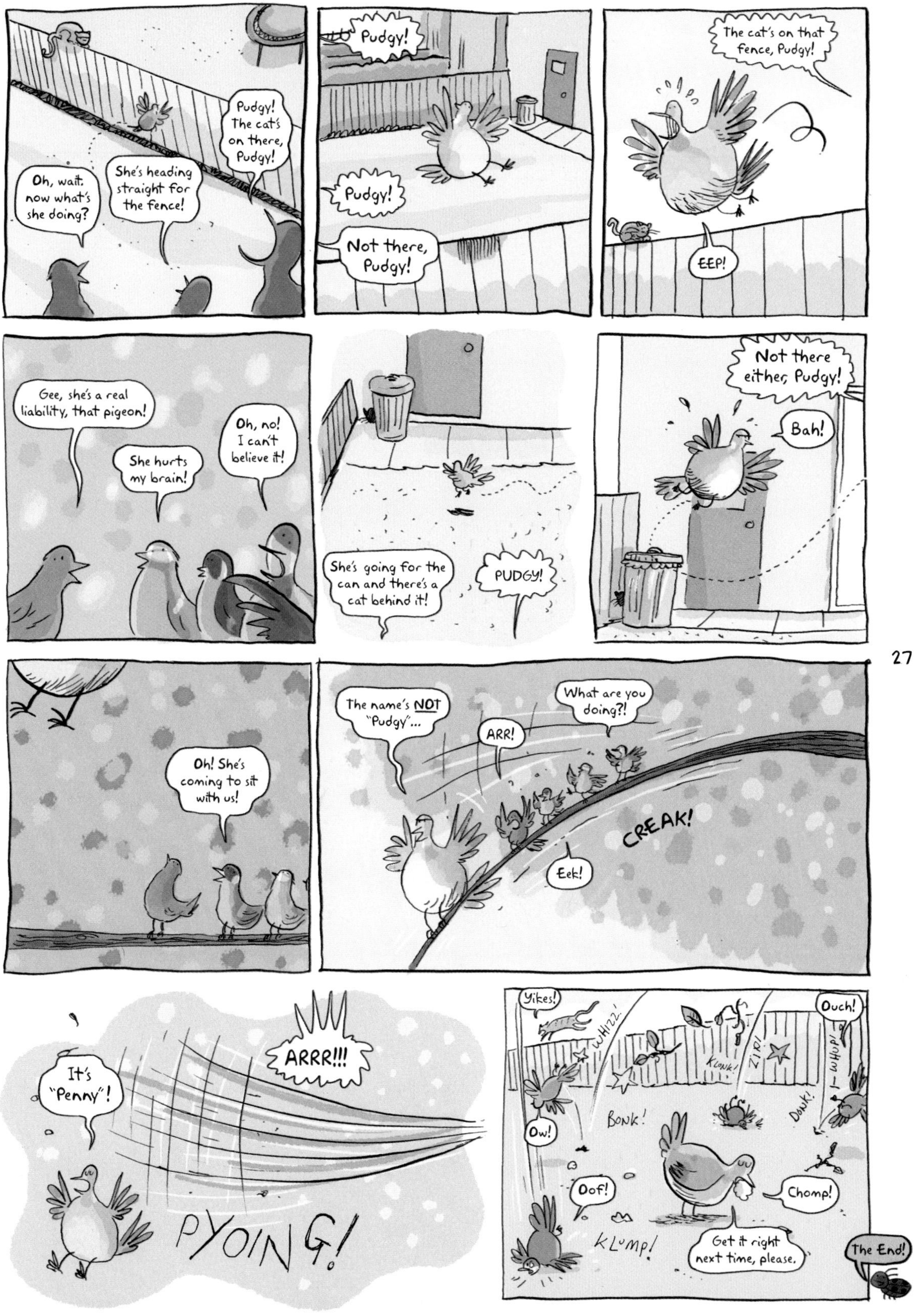
Oh, wait. now what's she doing?
She's heading straight for the fence!
Pudgy! The cat's on there, Pudgy!
Pudgy!
Pudgy!
Not there, Pudgy!
The cat's on that fence, Pudgy!
EEP!
Gee, she's a real liability, that pigeon!
She hurts my brain!
Oh, no! I can't believe it!
She's going for the can and there's a cat behind it!
PUDGY!
Not there either, Pudgy!
Bah!
Oh! She's coming to sit with us!
The name's NOT "Pudgy"...
ARR!
What are you doing?!
CREAK!
Eek!
It's "Penny"!
ARRR!!!
PYOING!
Yikes!
WHIZZ!
KLONK!
Ouch!
Ow!
BONK!
DONK!
Oof!
Chomp!
KLUMP!
Get it right next time, please.
The End!

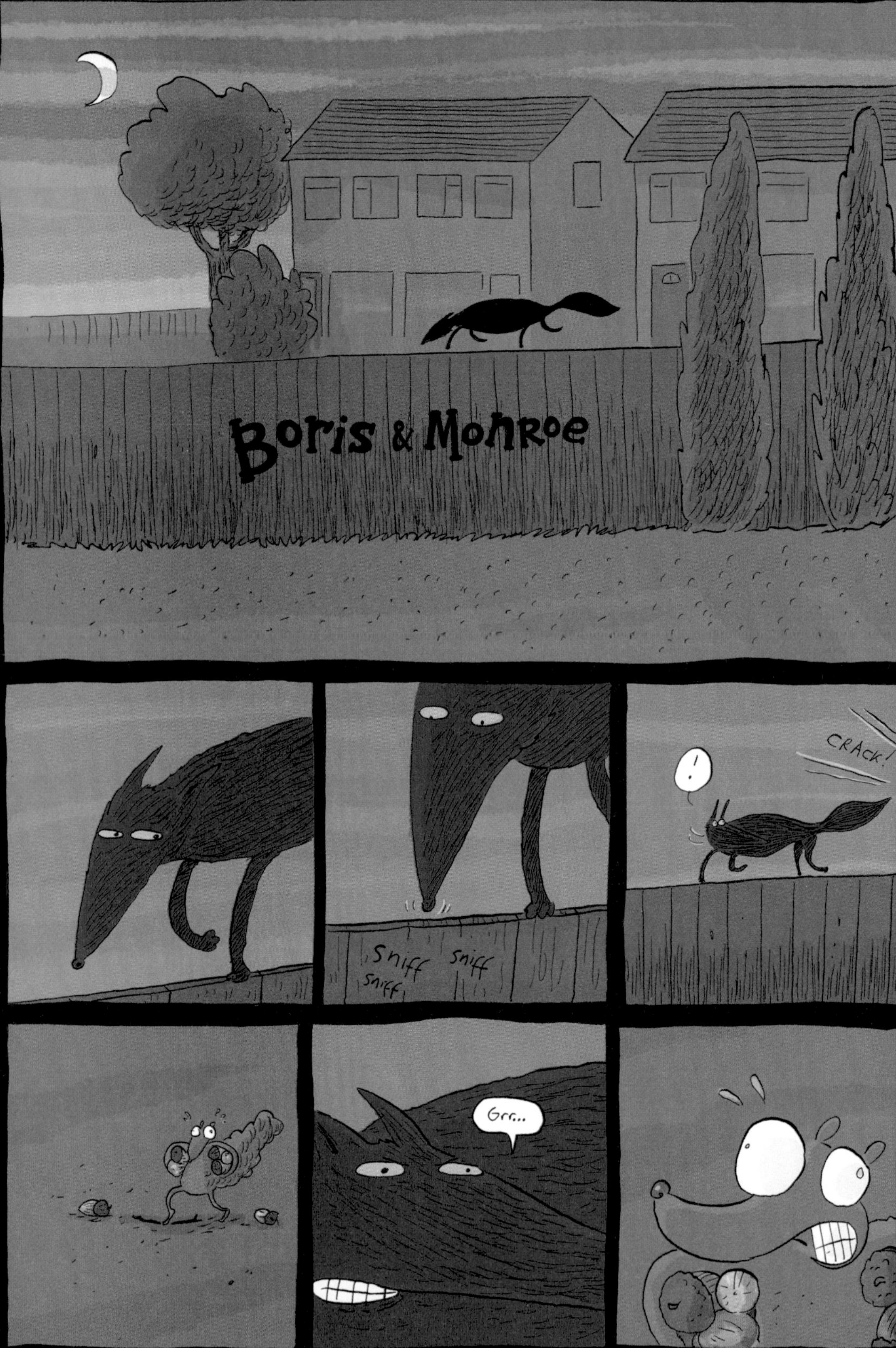
Boris & Monroe
Sniff sniff sniff
!
CRACK!
Grr...

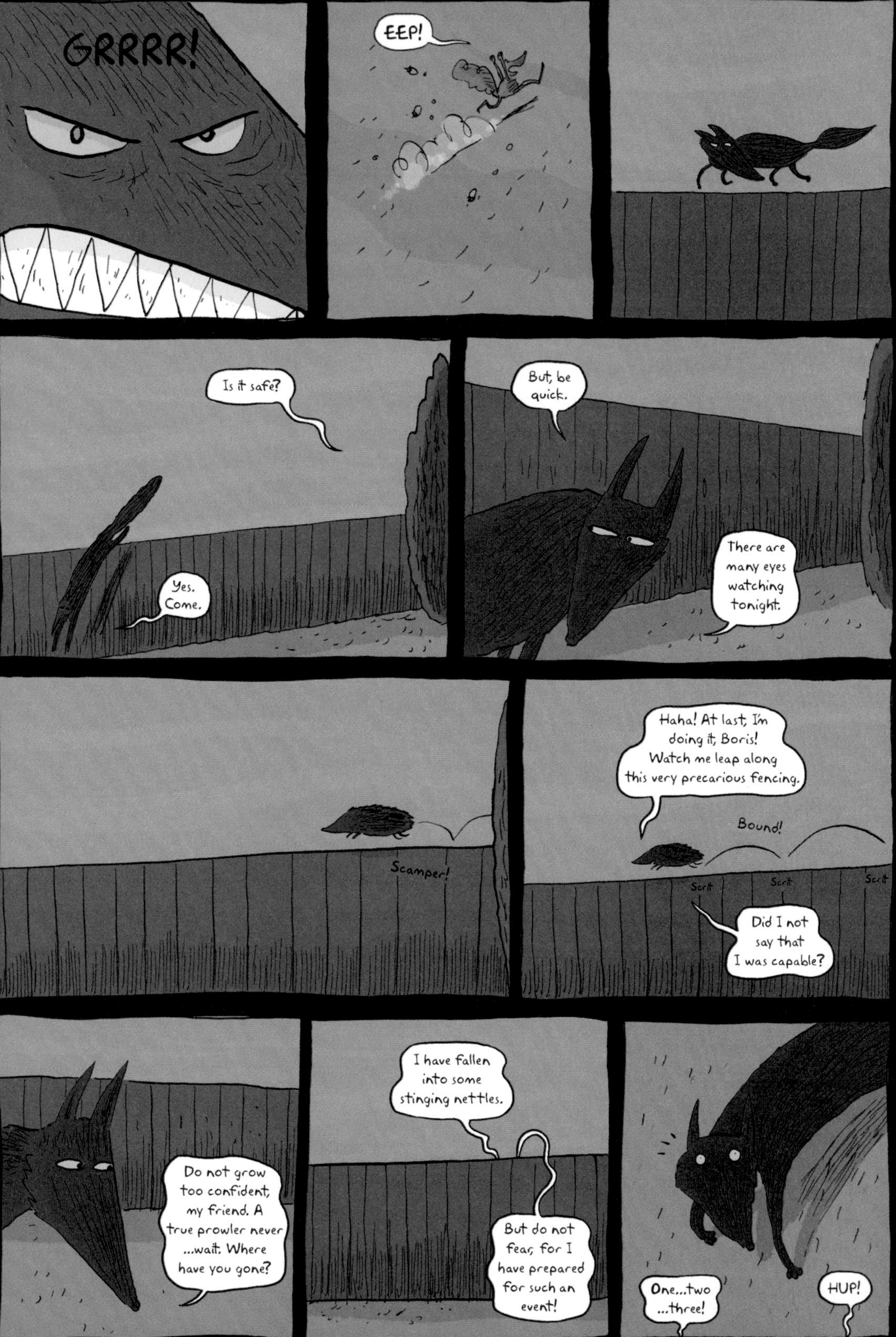
GRRRR!
EEP!
Is it safe?
Yes. Come.
But, be quick.
There are many eyes watching tonight.
Scamper!
Haha! At last, I'm doing it, Boris! Watch me leap along this very precarious fencing.
Bound!
Scrit
Scrit
Scrit
Did I not say that I was capable?
Do not grow too confident, my friend. A true prowler never ...wait. Where have you gone?
I have fallen into some stinging nettles.
But do not fear, for I have prepared for such an event!
One...two ...three!
HUP!

29

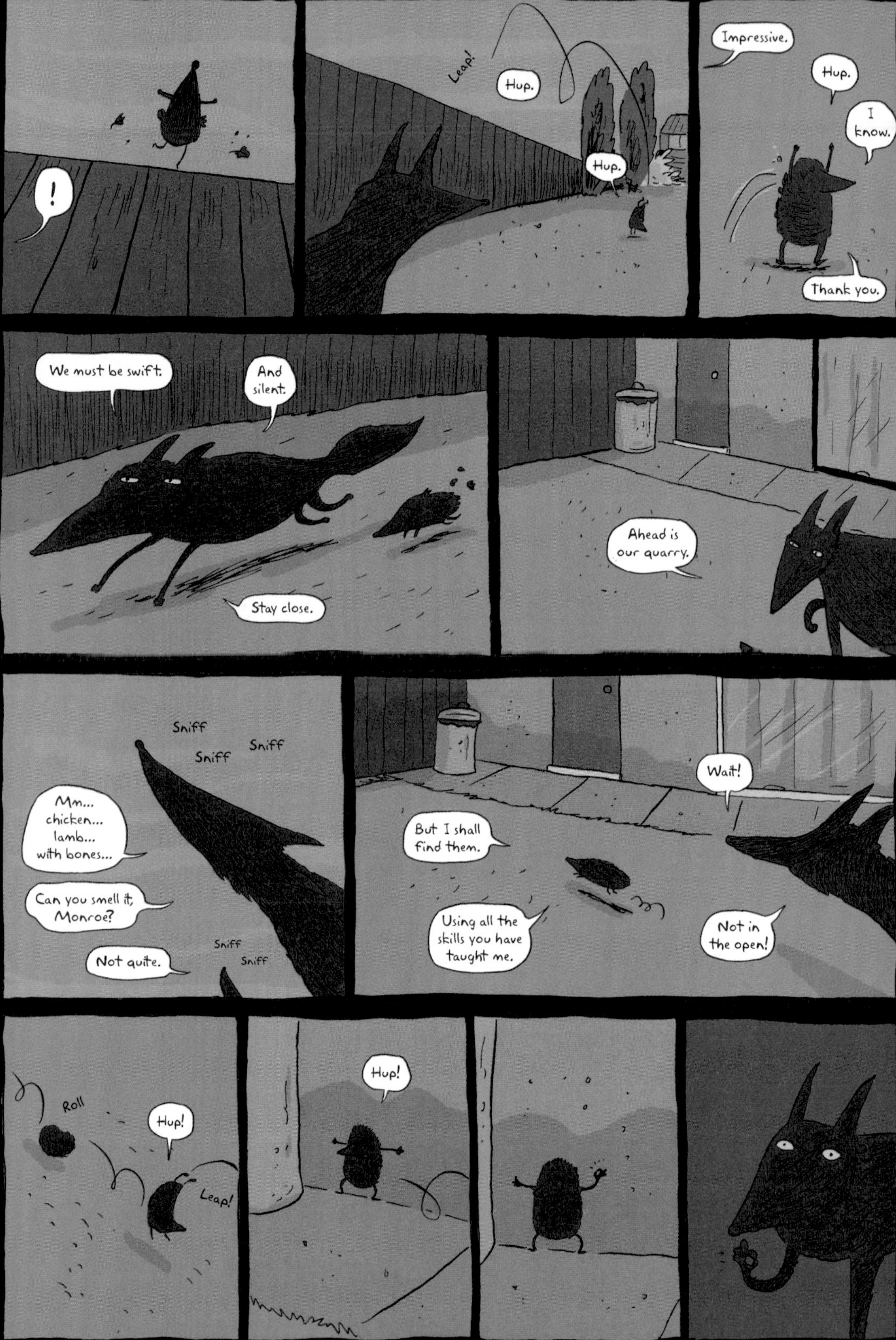
!
Leap!
Hup.
Hup.
Impressive.
Hup.
I know.
Thank you.
We must be swift.
And silent.
Stay close.
Ahead is our quarry.
Sniff
Sniff
Sniff
Mm... chicken... lamb... with bones...
Can you smell it, Monroe?
Not quite.
Sniff
Sniff
Wait!
But I shall find them.
Using all the skills you have taught me.
Not in the open!
Roll
Hup!
Leap!
Hup!

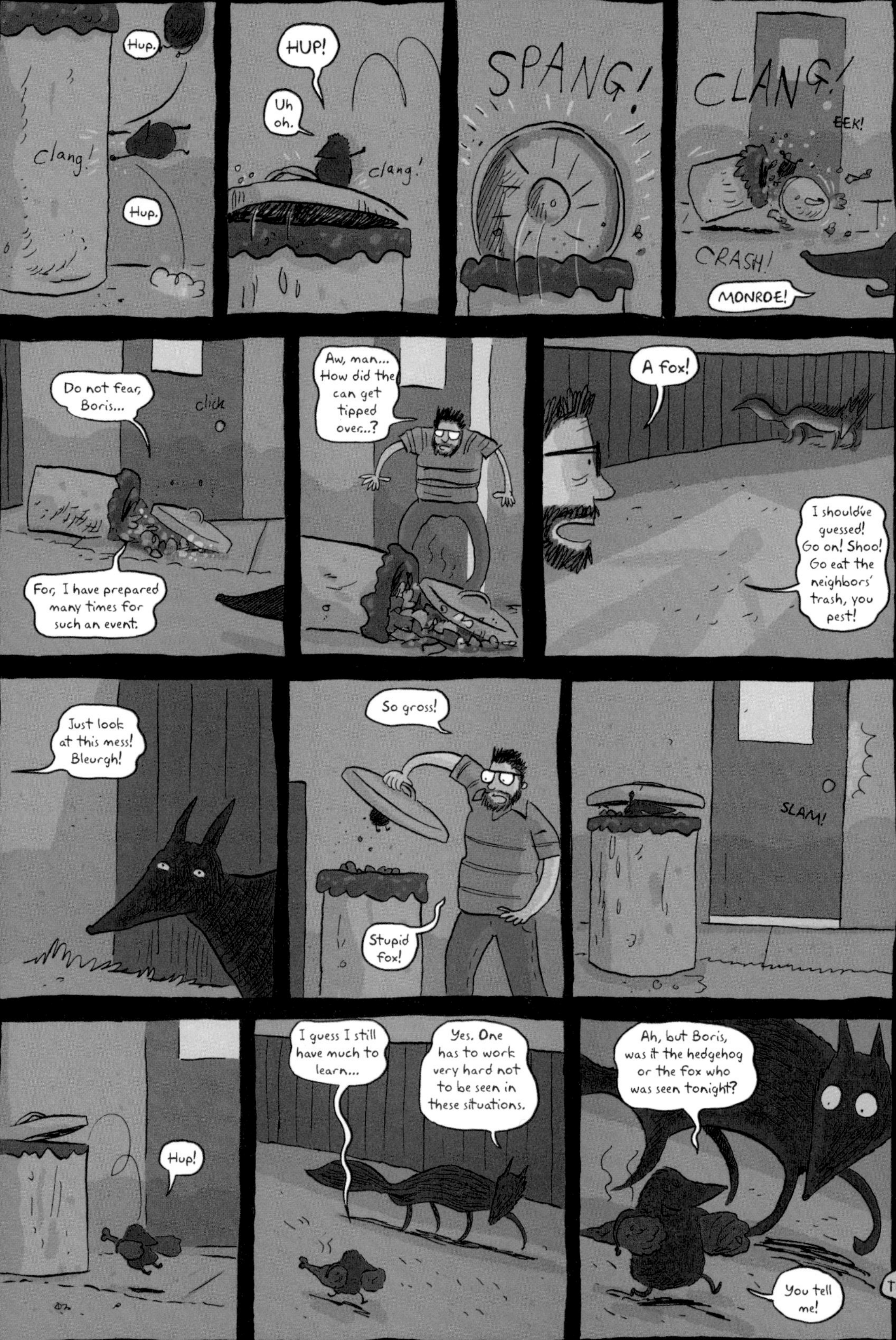

Hup.
Clang!
Hup.
HUP!
Uh oh.
clang!
SPANG!
CLANG!
EEK!
CRASH!
MONROE!
Do not fear, Boris...
click
For, I have prepared many times for such an event.
Aw, man... How did the can get tipped over...?
A fox!
I should've guessed! Go on! Shoo! Go eat the neighbors' trash, you pest!
Just look at this mess! Bleurgh!
So gross!
Stupid fox!
SLAM!
Hup!
I guess I still have much to learn...
Yes. One has to work very hard not to be seen in these situations.
Ah, but Boris, was it the hedgehog or the fox who was seen tonight?
You tell me!
The End!

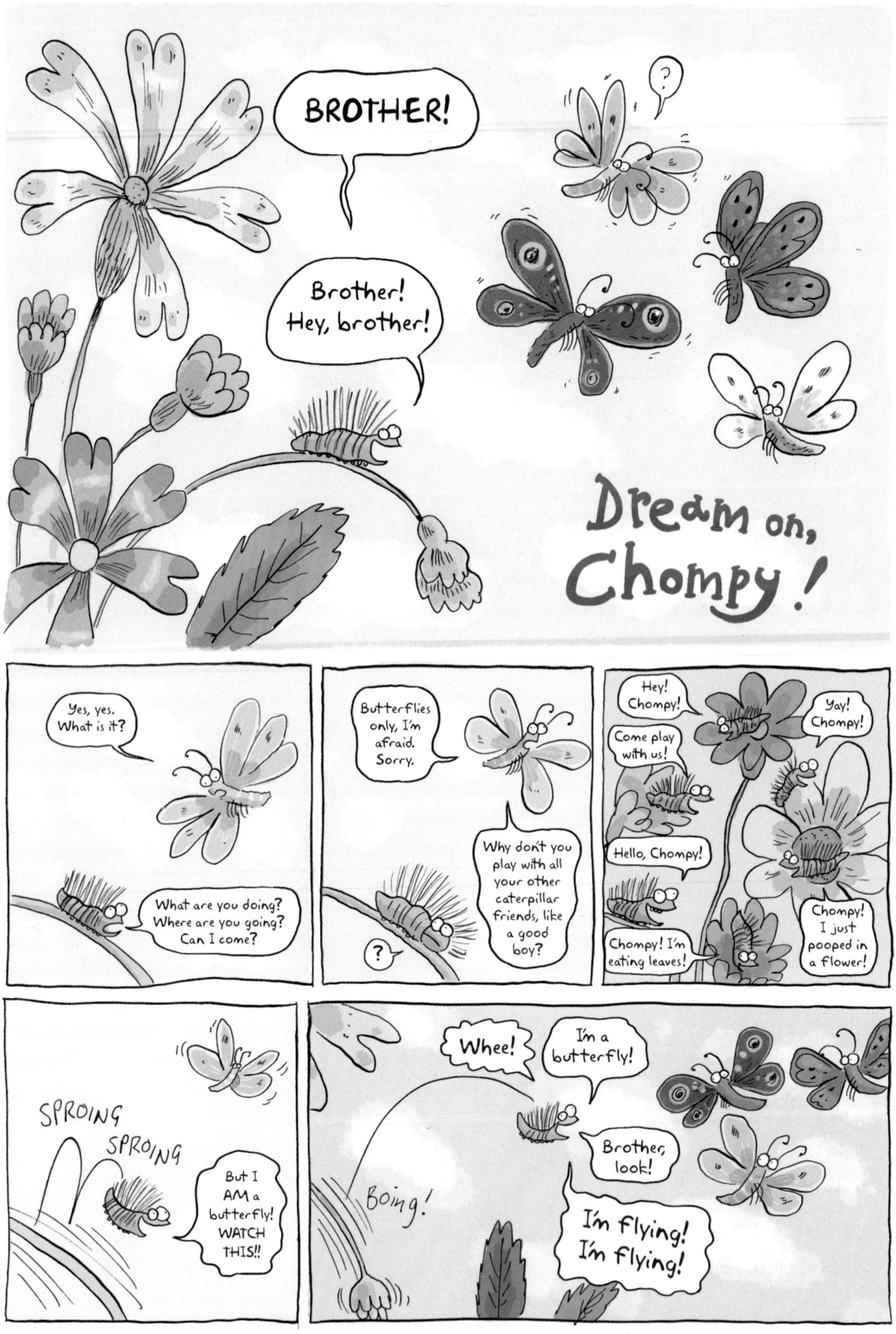
BROTHER!
?
Brother! Hey, brother!
Dream on, Chompy!
Yes, yes. What is it?
What are you doing? Where are you going? Can I come?
Butterflies only, I'm afraid. Sorry.
?
Why don't you play with all your other caterpillar friends, like a good boy?
Hey! Chompy!
Come play with us!
Yay! Chompy!
Hello, Chompy!
Chompy! I'm eating leaves!
Chompy! I just pooped in a flower!
SPROING
SPROING
But I AM a butterfly! WATCH THIS!!
Whee!
I'm a butterfly!
Brother, look!
Boing!
I'm flying! I'm flying!

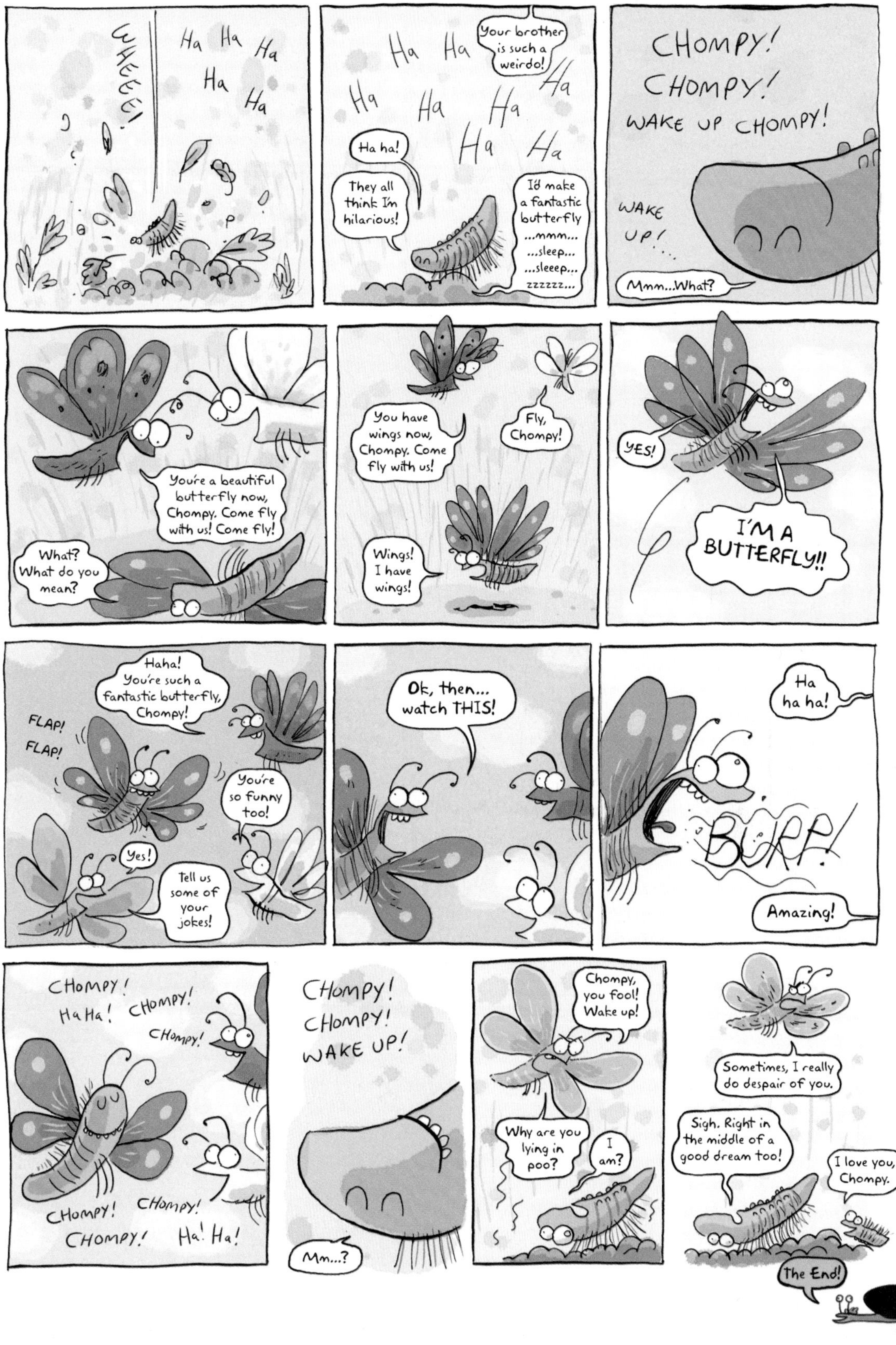
WHEEEE!
Ha Ha Ha Ha Ha
Ha Ha Ha Ha Ha Ha Ha Ha
Your brother is such a weirdo!
Ha ha!
They all think I'm hilarious!
I'd make a fantastic butterfly ...mmm... ...sleep... ...sleeep... zzzzzz...
CHOMPY! CHOMPY! WAKE UP CHOMPY!
WAKE UP!
Mmm...What?
You're a beautiful butterfly now, Chompy. Come fly with us! Come fly!
What? What do you mean?
You have wings now, Chompy. Come fly with us!
Fly, Chompy!
Wings! I have wings!
YES!
I'M A BUTTERFLY!!
Haha! You're such a fantastic butterfly, Chompy!
FLAP! FLAP!
You're so funny too!
Yes!
Tell us some of your jokes!
Ok, then... watch THIS!
Ha ha ha!
BURP!
Amazing!
CHOMPY! HaHa! CHOMPY! CHOMPY!
CHOMPY! CHOMPY! CHOMPY! Ha! Ha!
CHOMPY! CHOMPY! WAKE UP!
Mm...?
Chompy, you fool! Wake up!
Why are you lying in poo?
I am?
Sometimes, I really do despair of you.
Sigh. Right in the middle of a good dream too!
I love you, Chompy.
The End!

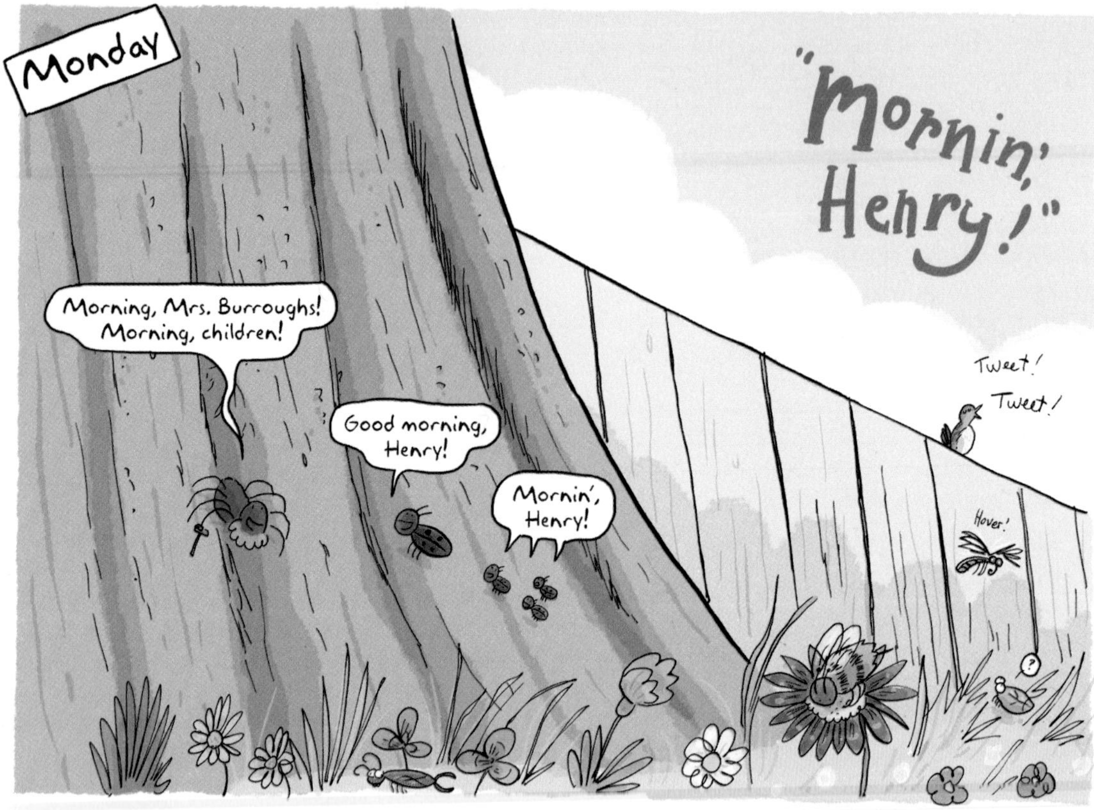
Monday
"Mornin', Henry!"
Morning, Mrs. Burroughs! Morning, children!
Good morning, Henry!
Mornin', Henry!
Tweet! Tweet!
Hover!
?

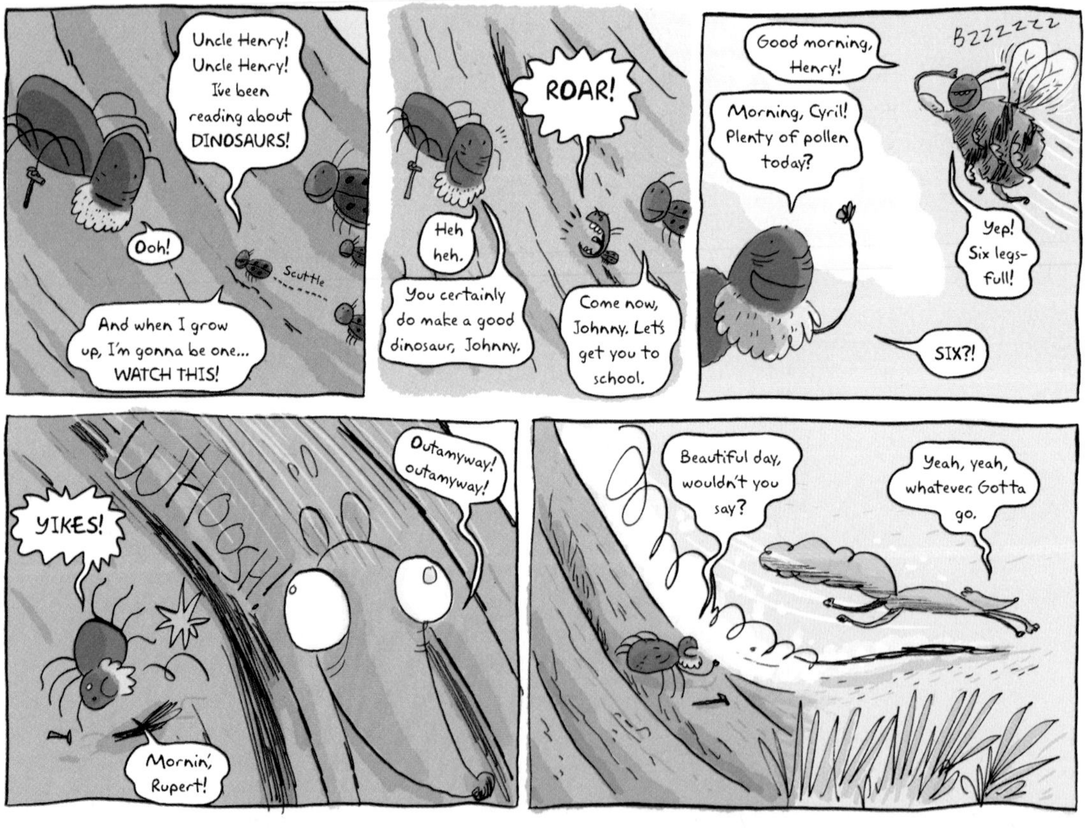
Uncle Henry! Uncle Henry! I've been reading about DINOSAURS!
Ooh!
Scuttle
And when I grow up, I'm gonna be one... WATCH THIS!
ROAR!
Heh heh.
You certainly do make a good dinosaur, Johnny.
Come now, Johnny. Let's get you to school.
Good morning, Henry!
BZZZZZZ
Morning, Cyril! Plenty of pollen today?
Yep! Six legs-full!
SIX?!
YIKES!
WHOOSH!
Outamyway! outamyway!
Mornin', Rupert!
Beautiful day, wouldn't you say?
Yeah, yeah, whatever. Gotta go.

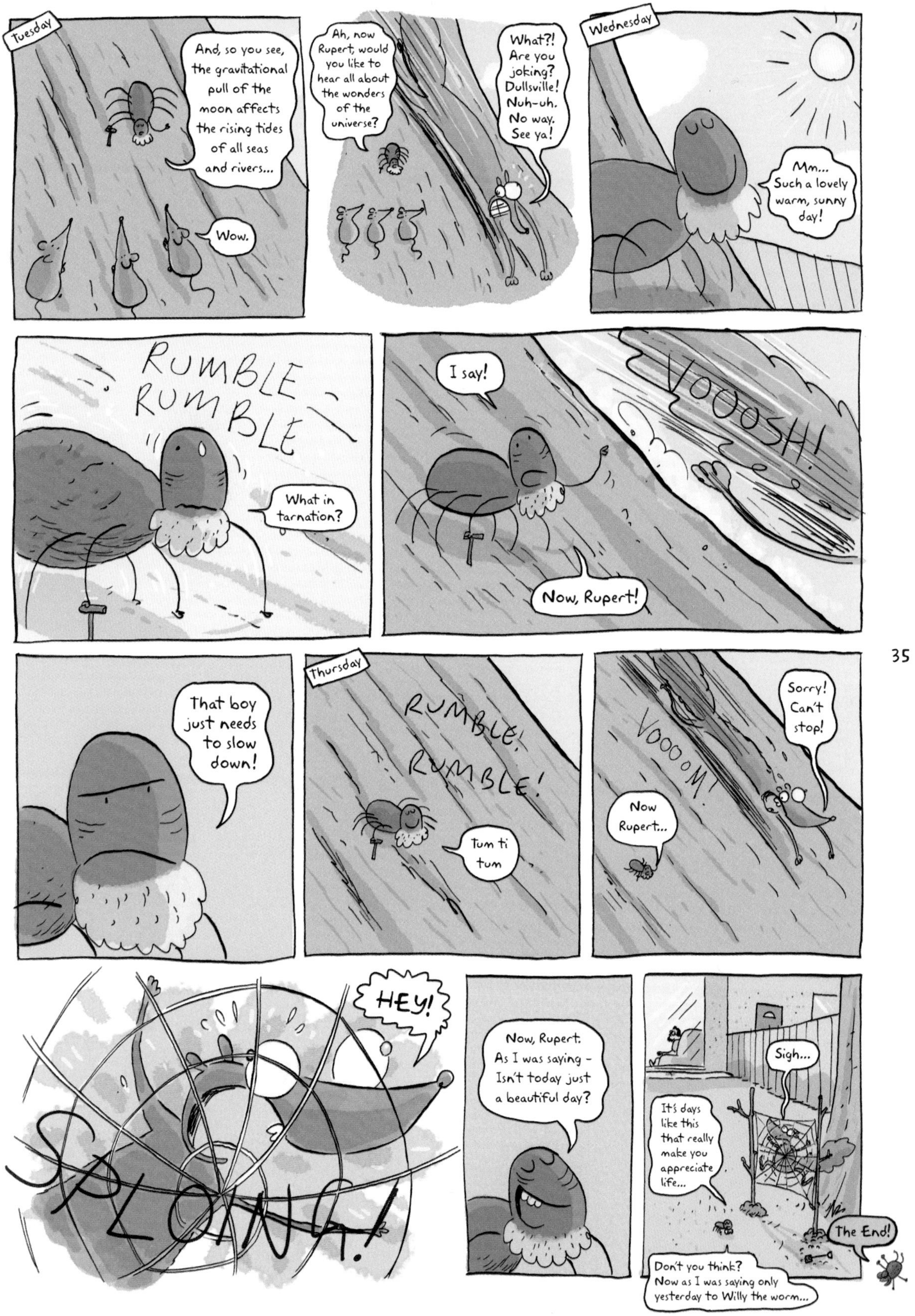
Tuesday
And, so you see, the gravitational pull of the moon affects the rising tides of all seas and rivers...
Wow.
Ah, now Rupert, would you like to hear all about the wonders of the universe?
What?! Are you joking? Dullsville! Nuh-uh. No way. See ya!
Wednesday
Mm... Such a lovely warm, sunny day!
RUMBLE RUMBLE
What in tarnation?
I say!
VOOOSH!
Now, Rupert!
That boy just needs to slow down!
Thursday
RUMBLE! RUMBLE!
Tum ti tum
VOOOOM!
Sorry! Can't stop!
Now Rupert...
HEY!
SPLONG!
Now, Rupert. As I was saying - Isn't today just a beautiful day?
Sigh...
It's days like this that really make you appreciate life...
Don't you think? Now as I was saying only yesterday to Willy the worm...
The End!

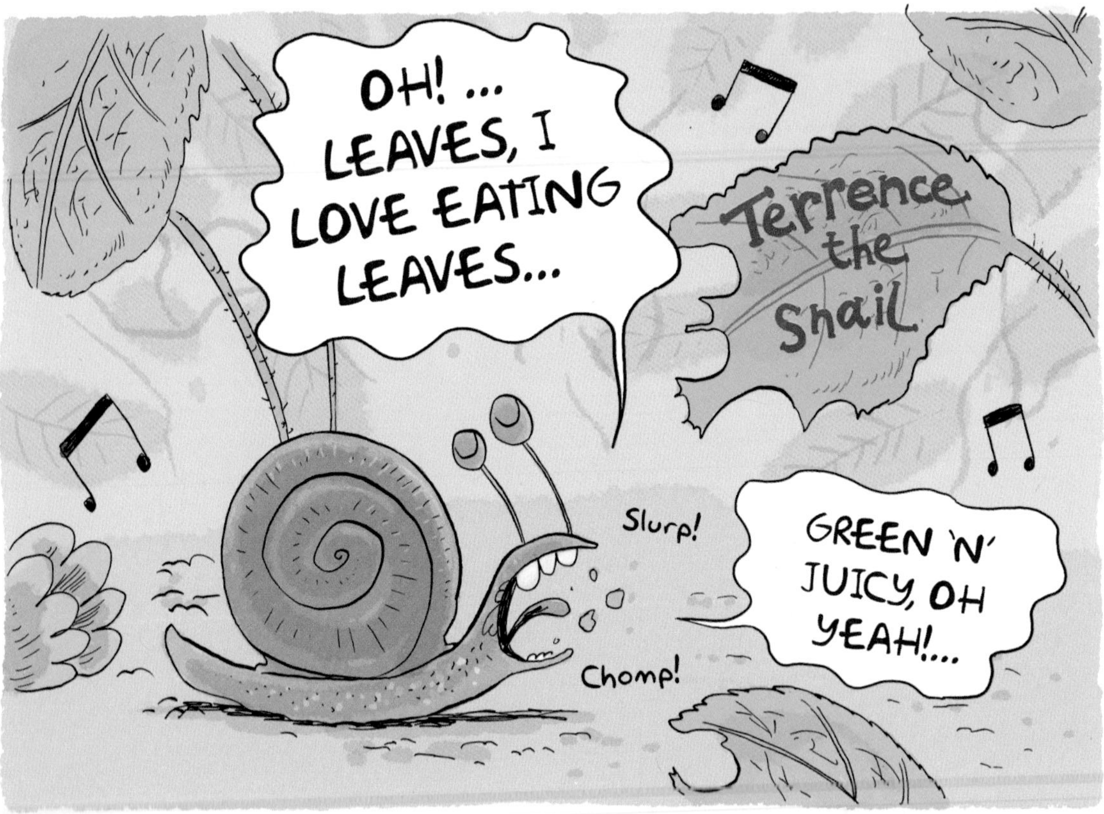
OH! ... LEAVES, I LOVE EATING LEAVES...
Terrence the Snail
Slurp!
GREEN 'N' JUICY, OH YEAH!...
Chomp!

36

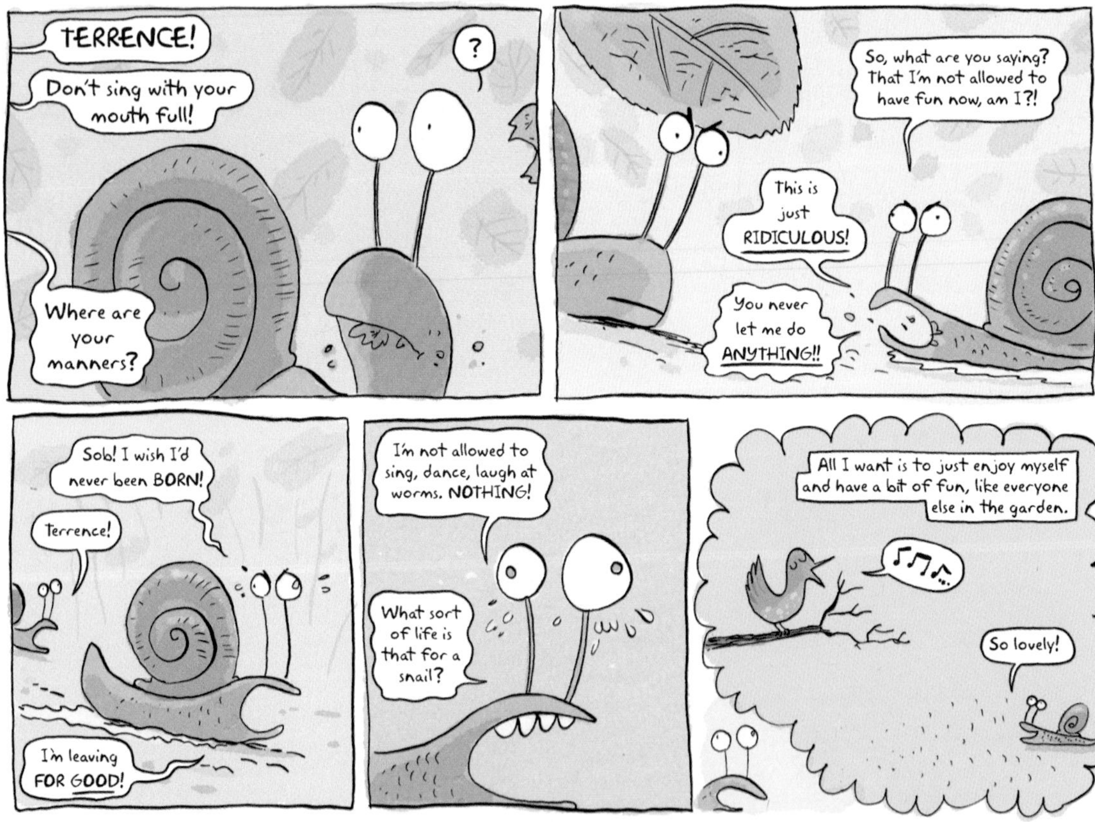
TERRENCE!
Don't sing with your mouth full!
?
Where are your manners?
So, what are you saying? That I'm not allowed to have fun now, am I?!
This is just RIDICULOUS!
You never let me do ANYTHING!!
Sob! I wish I'd never been BORN!
Terrence!
I'm leaving FOR GOOD!
I'm not allowed to sing, dance, laugh at worms. NOTHING!
What sort of life is that for a snail?
All I want is to just enjoy myself and have a bit of fun, like everyone else in the garden.
So lovely!

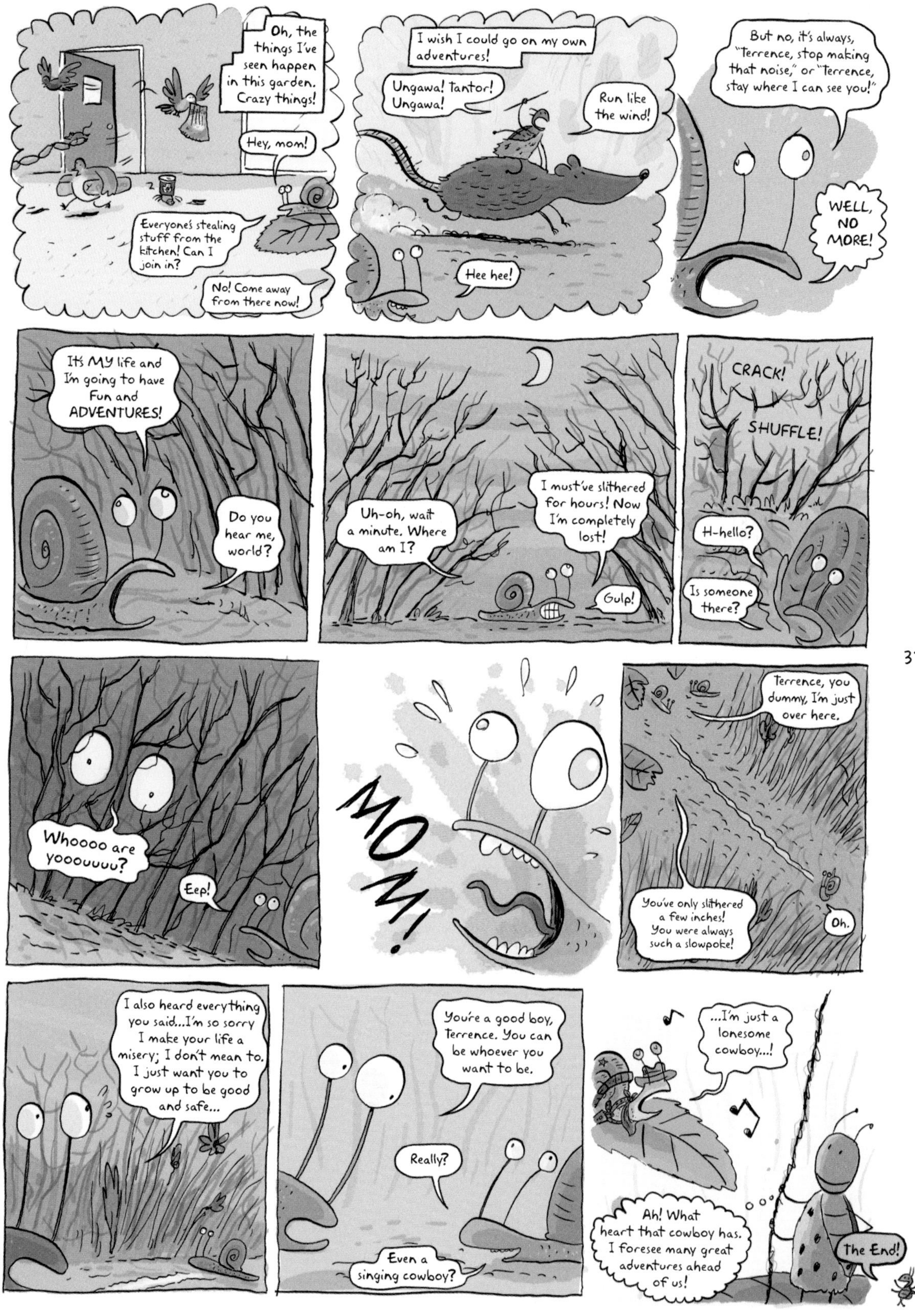

Oh, the things I've seen happen in this garden. Crazy things!
Hey, mom!
Everyone's stealing stuff from the kitchen! Can I join in?
No! Come away from there now!
I wish I could go on my own adventures!
Ungawa! Tantor! Ungawa!
Run like the wind!
Hee hee!
But no, it's always, "Terrence, stop making that noise," or "Terrence, stay where I can see you!"
WELL, NO MORE!
It's MY life and I'm going to have Fun and ADVENTURES!
Do you hear me, world?
Uh-oh, wait a minute. Where am I?
I must've slithered for hours! Now I'm completely lost!
Gulp!
CRACK!
SHUFFLE!
H-hello?
Is someone there?
Whoooo are yooouuuu?
Eep!
MOM!
Terrence, you dummy, I'm just over here.
You've only slithered a few inches! You were always such a slowpoke!
Oh.
I also heard everything you said...I'm so sorry I make your life a misery; I don't mean to. I just want you to grow up to be good and safe...
You're a good boy, Terrence. You can be whoever you want to be.
Really?
Even a singing cowboy?
...I'm just a lonesome cowboy...!
Ah! What heart that cowboy has. I foresee many great adventures ahead of us!
The End!

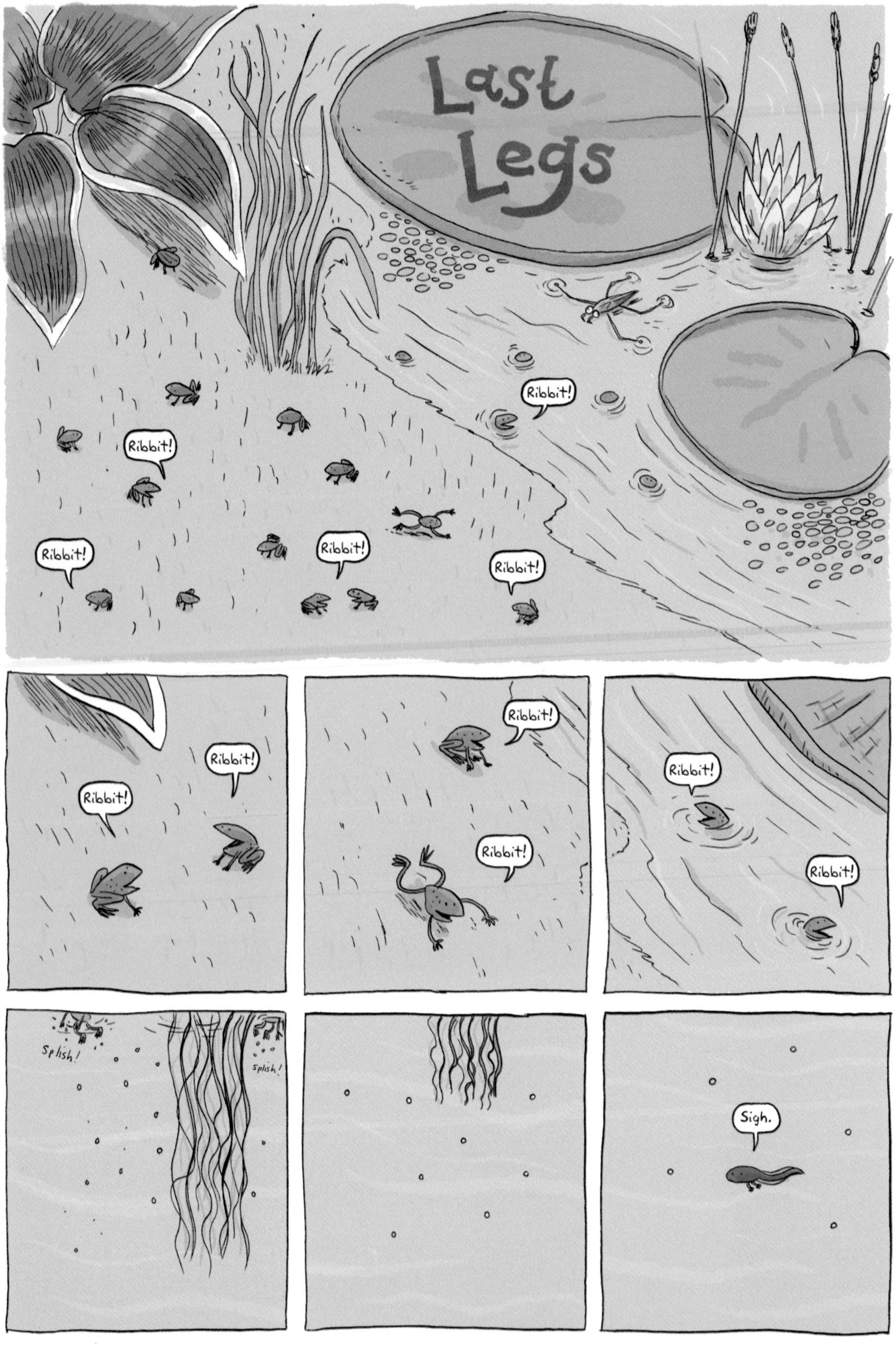

Last Legs
Ribbit!
Ribbit!
Ribbit!
Ribbit!
Ribbit!
Ribbit!
Ribbit!
Ribbit!
Ribbit!
Ribbit!
Ribbit!
Splish!
Splish!
Sigh.

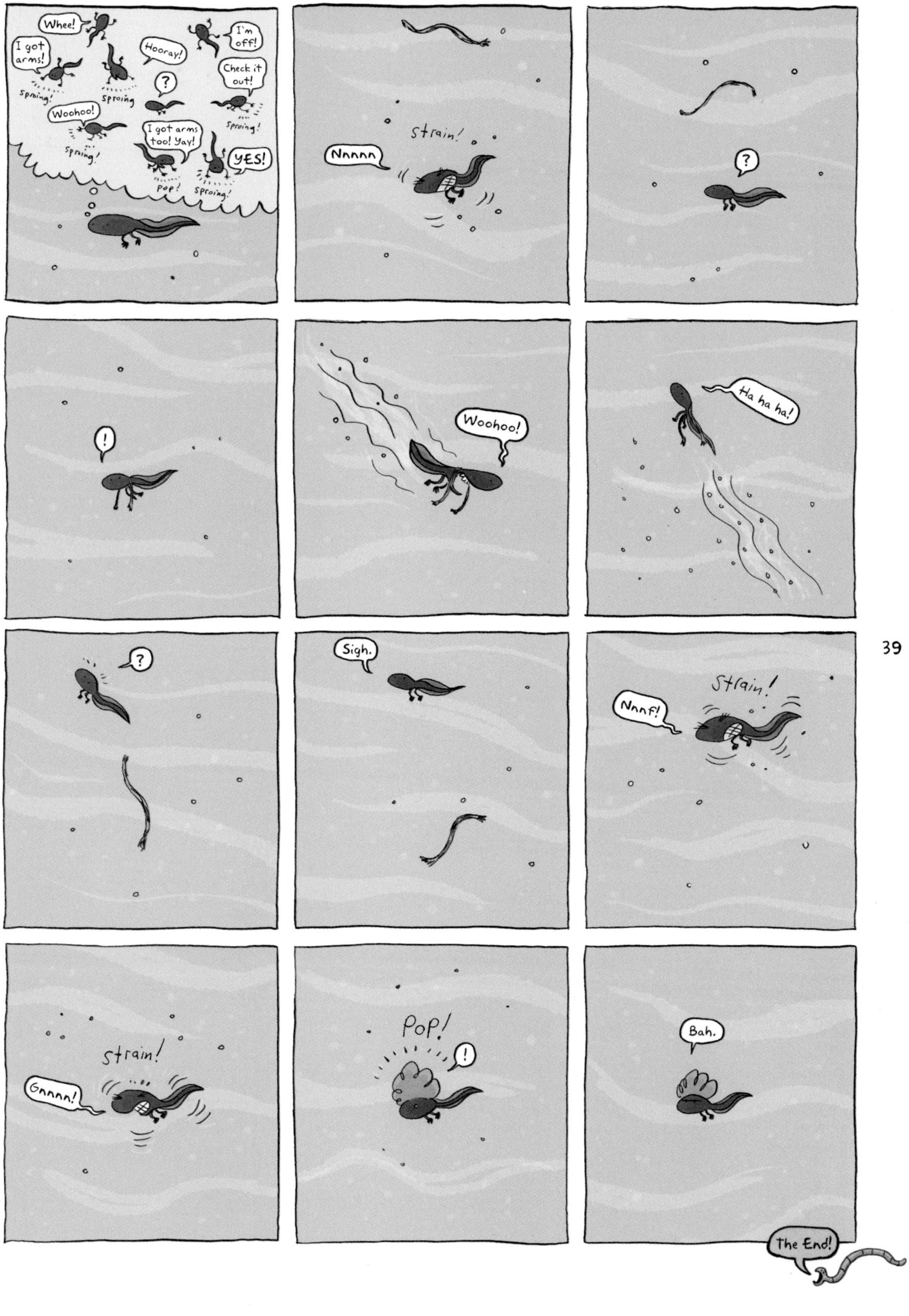
Whee!
I'm off!
I got arms!
Hooray!
Check it out!
?
Sproing!
Sproing
Sproing!
Woohoo!
Sproing!
I got arms too! Yay!
YES!
Pop!
Sproing!
Nnnnn
Strain!
?
!
Woohoo!
Ha ha ha!
?
Sigh.
Nnnf!
Strain!
Gnnnn!
strain!
POP!
!
Bah.
The End!

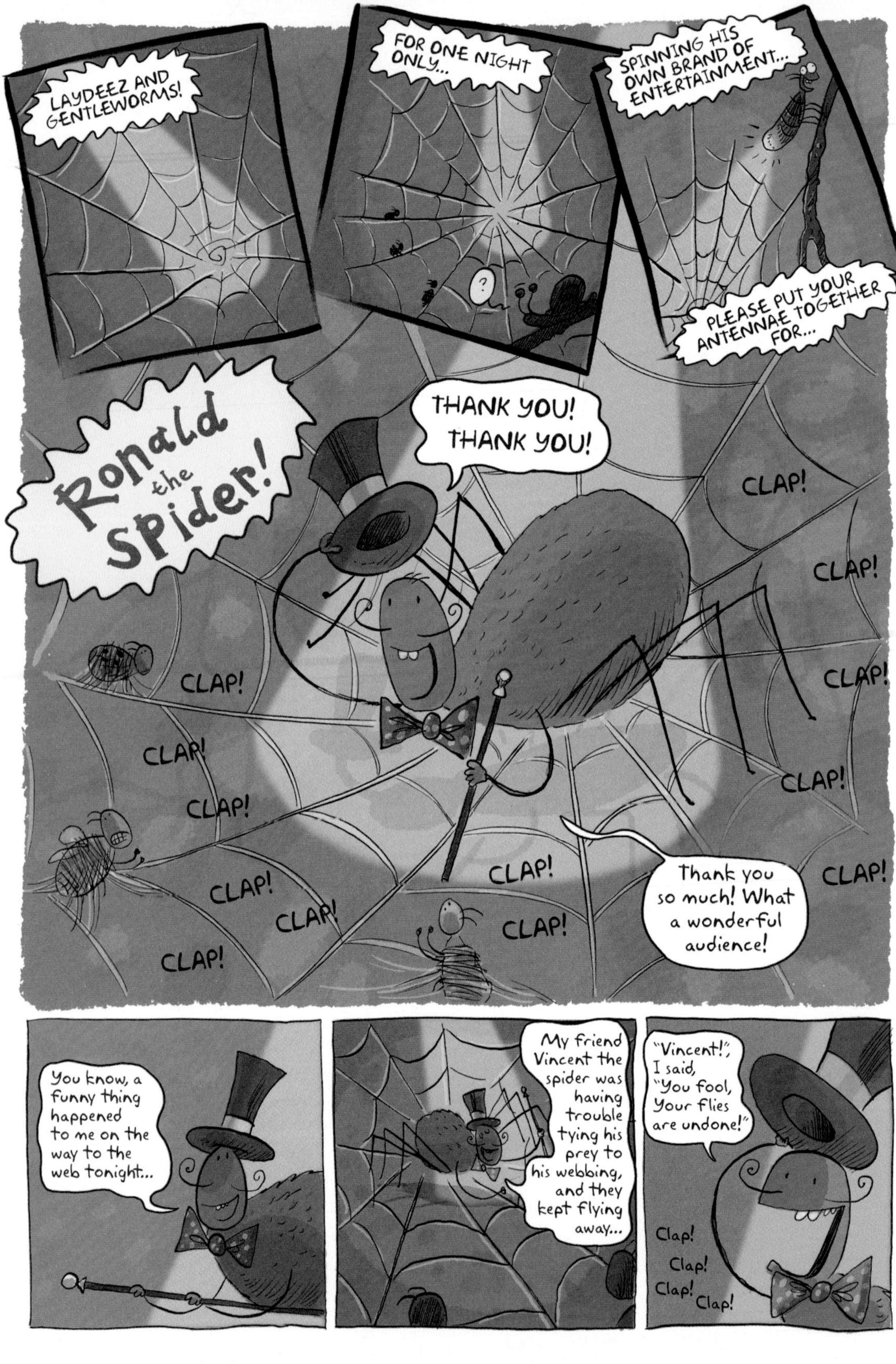
LAYDEEZ AND GENTLEWORMS!
FOR ONE NIGHT ONLY...
?
SPINNING HIS OWN BRAND OF ENTERTAINMENT...
PLEASE PUT YOUR ANTENNAE TOGETHER FOR...
Ronald the Spider!
THANK YOU! THANK YOU!
CLAP!
CLAP!
CLAP!
CLAP!
CLAP!
CLAP!
CLAP!
CLAP!
CLAP!
CLAP!
CLAP!
CLAP!
CLAP!
Thank you so much! What a wonderful audience!
You know, a funny thing happened to me on the way to the web tonight...
My friend Vincent the spider was having trouble tying his prey to his webbing, and they kept flying away...
"Vincent!", I said, "You fool, Your flies are undone!"
Clap!
Clap!
Clap!
Clap!

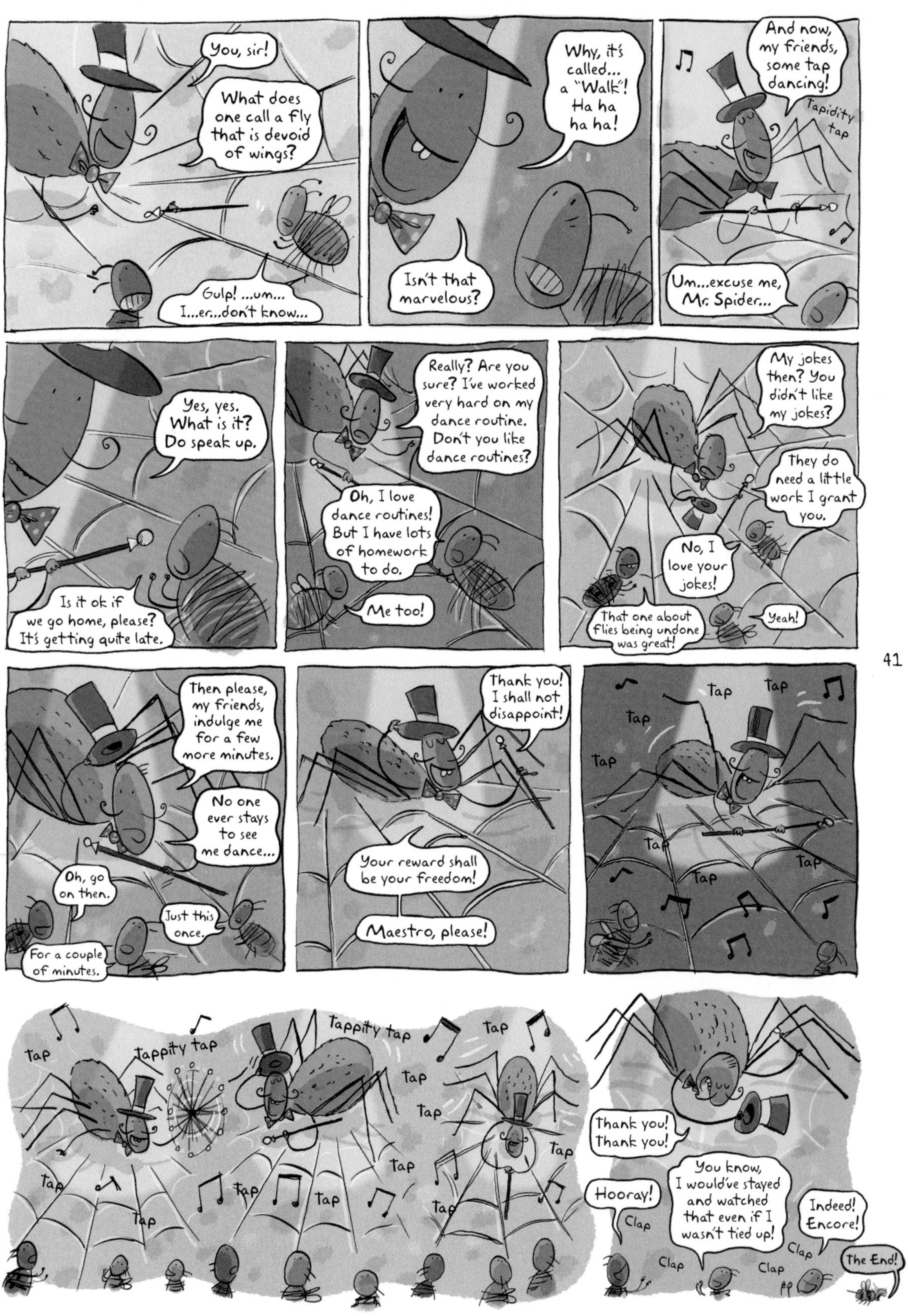
You, sir!
What does one call a fly that is devoid of wings?
Gulp! ...um... I...er...don't know...
Why, it's called... a "Walk"! Ha ha ha ha!
Isn't that marvelous?
And now, my friends, some tap dancing!
Tapidity tap
Um...excuse me, Mr. Spider...
Yes, yes. What is it? Do speak up.
Is it ok if we go home, please? It's getting quite late.
Really? Are you sure? I've worked very hard on my dance routine. Don't you like dance routines?
Oh, I love dance routines! But I have lots of homework to do.
Me too!
My jokes then? You didn't like my jokes?
They do need a little work I grant you.
No, I love your jokes!
That one about flies being undone was great!
Yeah!
Then please, my friends, indulge me for a few more minutes.
No one ever stays to see me dance...
Oh, go on then.
Just this once.
For a couple of minutes.
Thank you! I shall not disappoint!
Your reward shall be your freedom!
Maestro, please!
Tap Tap Tap Tap Tap Tap Tap
tap tappity tap tappity tap Tap Tap Tap Tap Tap Tap Tap Tap Tap Tap
Thank you! Thank you!
Hooray!
Clap
You know, I would've stayed and watched that even if I wasn't tied up!
Clap Clap Clap
Indeed! Encore!
The End!

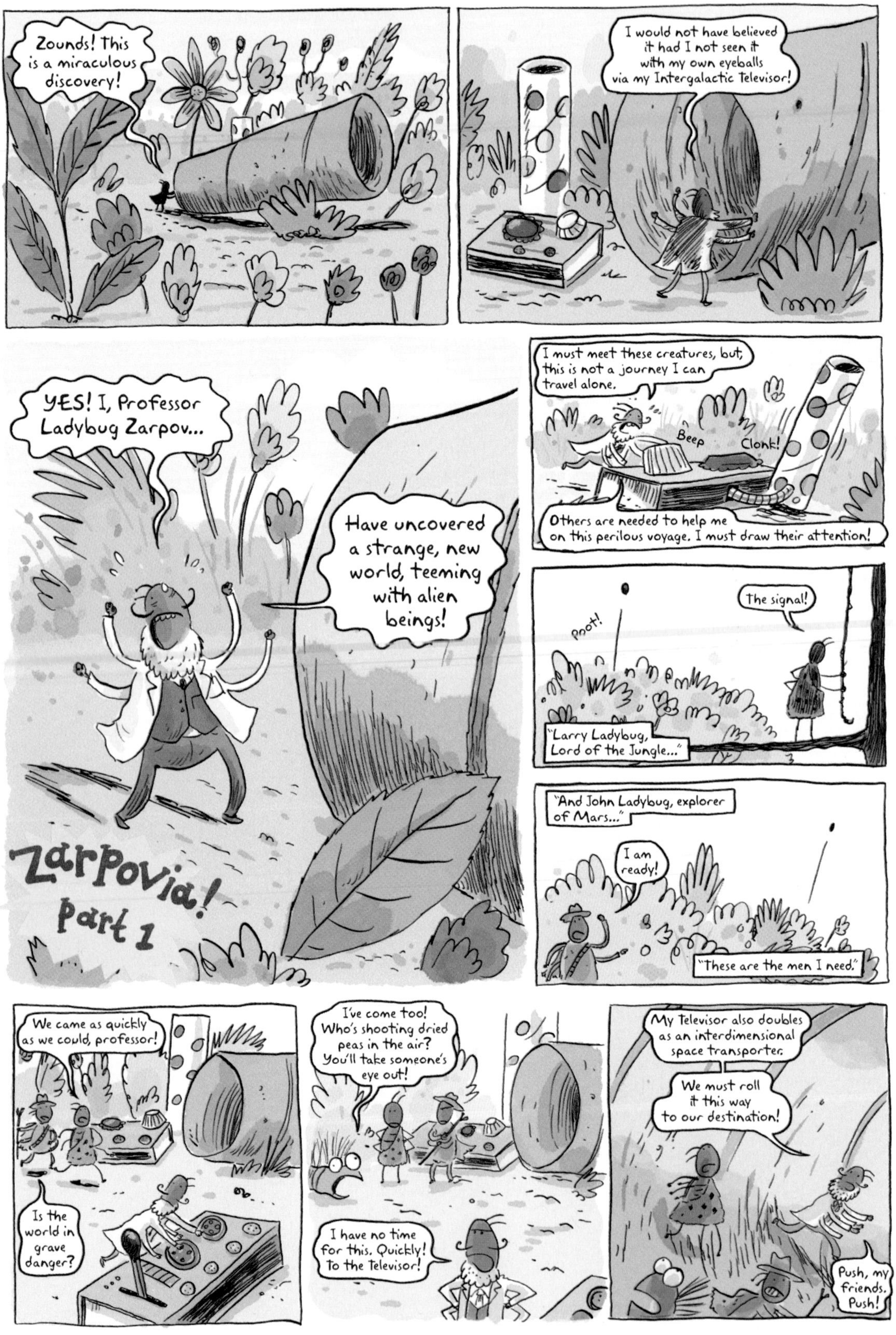

Zounds! This is a miraculous discovery!
I would not have believed it had I not seen it with my own eyeballs via my Intergalactic Televisor!
YES! I, Professor Ladybug Zarpov...
Have uncovered a strange, new world, teeming with alien beings!
Zarpovia! part 1
I must meet these creatures, but, this is not a journey I can travel alone.
Beep
Clonk!
Others are needed to help me on this perilous voyage. I must draw their attention!
poot!
The signal!
"Larry Ladybug, Lord of the Jungle..."
"And John Ladybug, explorer of Mars..."
I am ready!
"These are the men I need."
We came as quickly as we could, professor!
Is the world in grave danger?
I've come too! Who's shooting dried peas in the air? You'll take someone's eye out!
I have no time for this. Quickly! To the Televisor!
My Televisor also doubles as an interdimensional space transporter.
We must roll it this way to our destination!
Push, my friends. Push!

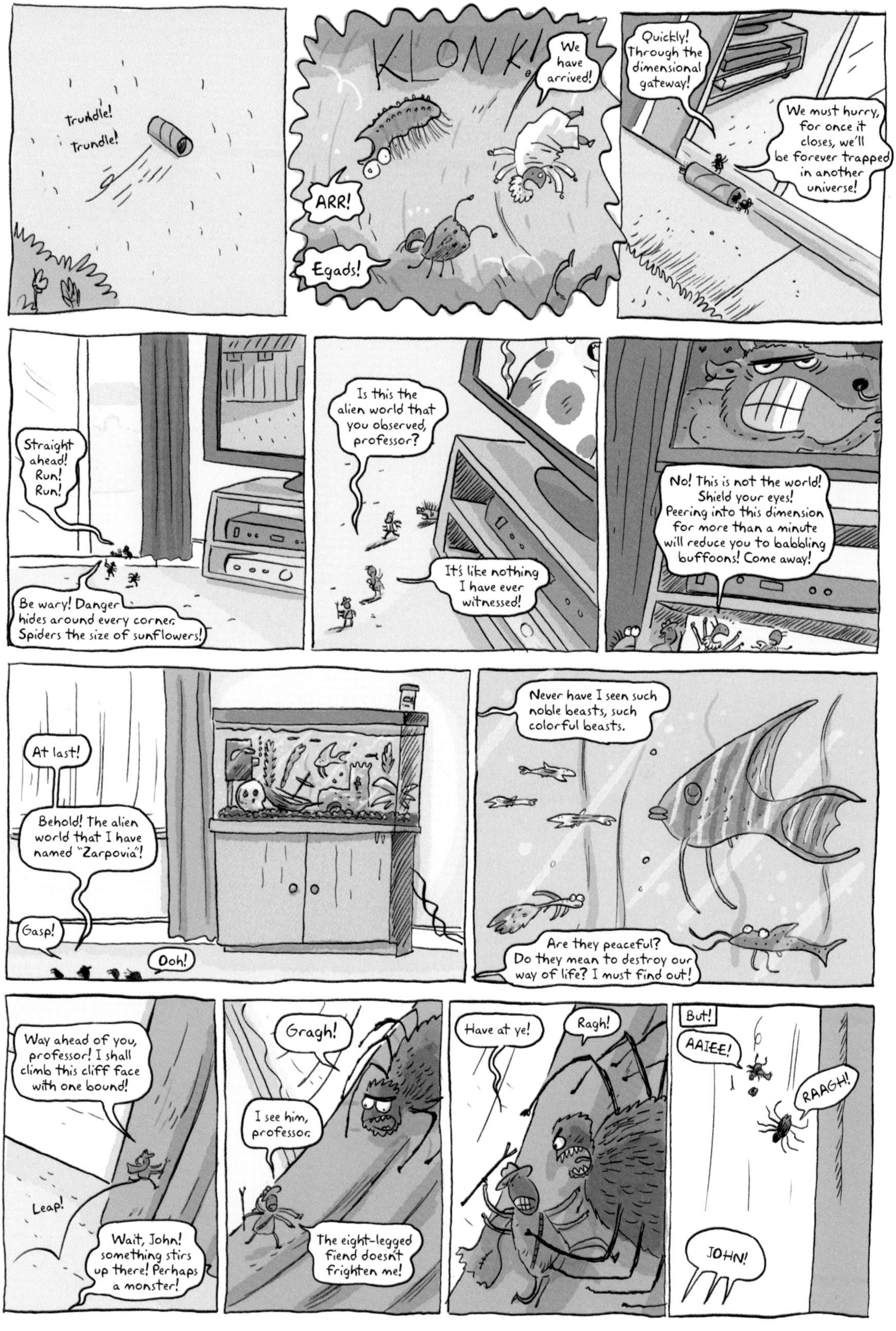
trundle!
trundle!
KLONK!
We have arrived!
ARR!
Egads!
Quickly! Through the dimensional gateway!
We must hurry, for once it closes, we'll be forever trapped in another universe!
Straight ahead! Run! Run!
Be wary! Danger hides around every corner. Spiders the size of sunflowers!
Is this the alien world that you observed, professor?
It's like nothing I have ever witnessed!
No! This is not the world! Shield your eyes! Peering into this dimension for more than a minute will reduce you to babbling buffoons! Come away!
At last!
Behold! The alien world that I have named "Zarpovia"!
Gasp!
Ooh!
Never have I seen such noble beasts, such colorful beasts.
Are they peaceful? Do they mean to destroy our way of life? I must find out!
Way ahead of you, professor! I shall climb this cliff face with one bound!
Leap!
Wait, John! something stirs up there! Perhaps a monster!
Gragh!
I see him, professor.
The eight-legged fiend doesn't frighten me!
Have at ye!
Ragh!
But!
AAIEE!
RAAGH!
JOHN!

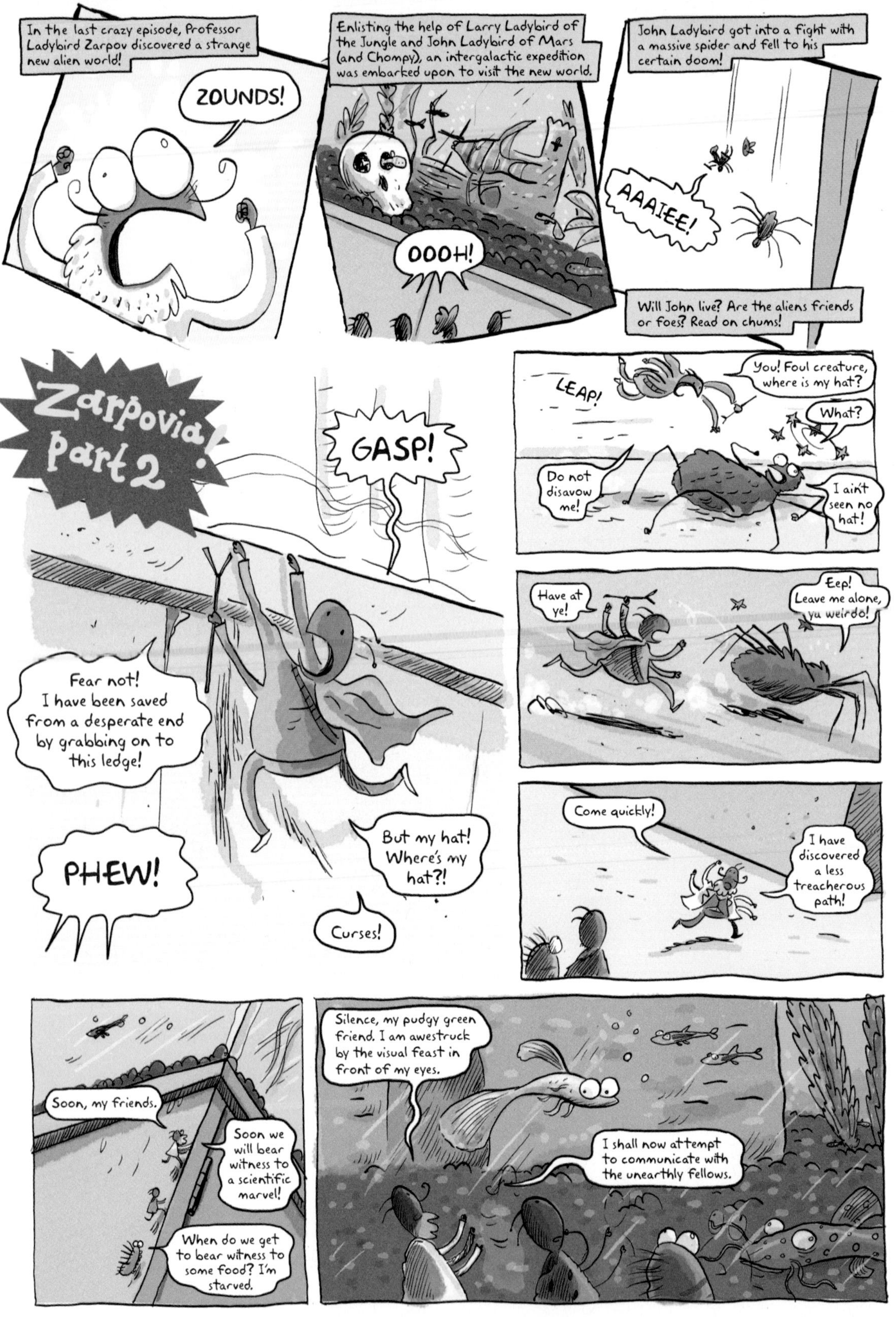

In the last crazy episode, Professor Ladybird Zarpov discovered a strange new alien world!
ZOUNDS!
Enlisting the help of Larry Ladybird of the Jungle and John Ladybird of Mars (and Chompy), an intergalactic expedition was embarked upon to visit the new world.
OOOH!
John Ladybird got into a fight with a massive spider and fell to his certain doom!
AAAIEE!
Will John live? Are the aliens friends or foes? Read on chums!
Zarpovia! part 2
GASP!
Fear not! I have been saved from a desperate end by grabbing on to this ledge!
PHEW!
But my hat! Where's my hat?!
Curses!
LEAP!
You! Foul creature, where is my hat?
What?
Do not disavow me!
I ain't seen no hat!
Have at ye!
Eep! Leave me alone, ya weirdo!
Come quickly!
I have discovered a less treacherous path!
Soon, my friends.
Soon we will bear witness to a scientific marvel!
When do we get to bear witness to some food? I'm starved.
Silence, my pudgy green friend. I am awestruck by the visual feast in front of my eyes.
I shall now attempt to communicate with the unearthly fellows.

44

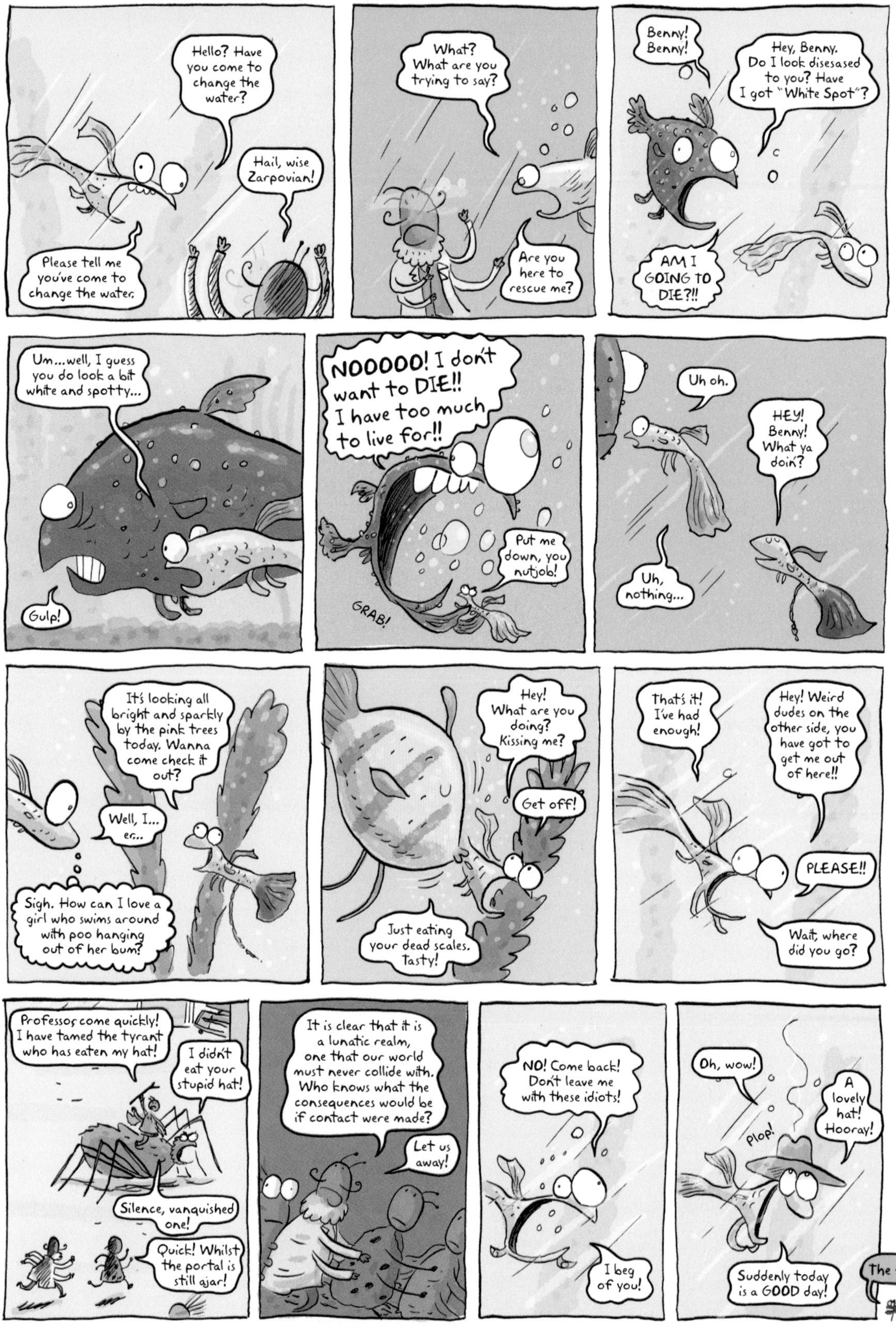
Hello? Have you come to change the water?
Hail, wise Zarpovian!
Please tell me you've come to change the water.
What? What are you trying to say?
Are you here to rescue me?
Benny! Benny!
Hey, Benny. Do I look disesased to you? Have I got "White Spot"?
AM I GOING TO DIE?!!
Um...well, I guess you do look a bit white and spotty...
Gulp!
NOOOOO! I don't want to DIE!! I have too much to live for!!
Put me down, you nutjob!
GRAB!
Uh oh.
HEY! Benny! What ya doin'?
Uh, nothing...
It's looking all bright and sparkly by the pink trees today. Wanna come check it out?
Well, I... er...
Sigh. How can I love a girl who swims around with poo hanging out of her bum?
Hey! What are you doing? Kissing me?
Get off!
Just eating your dead scales. Tasty!
That's it! I've had enough!
Hey! Weird dudes on the other side, you have got to get me out of here!!
PLEASE!!
Wait, where did you go?
Professor, come quickly! I have tamed the tyrant who has eaten my hat!
I didn't eat your stupid hat!
Silence, vanquished one!
Quick! Whilst the portal is still ajar!
It is clear that it is a lunatic realm, one that our world must never collide with. Who knows what the consequences would be if contact were made?
Let us away!
NO! Come back! Don't leave me with these idiots!
I beg of you!
Oh, wow!
A lovely hat! Hooray!
Plop!
Suddenly today is a GOOD day!
The End!

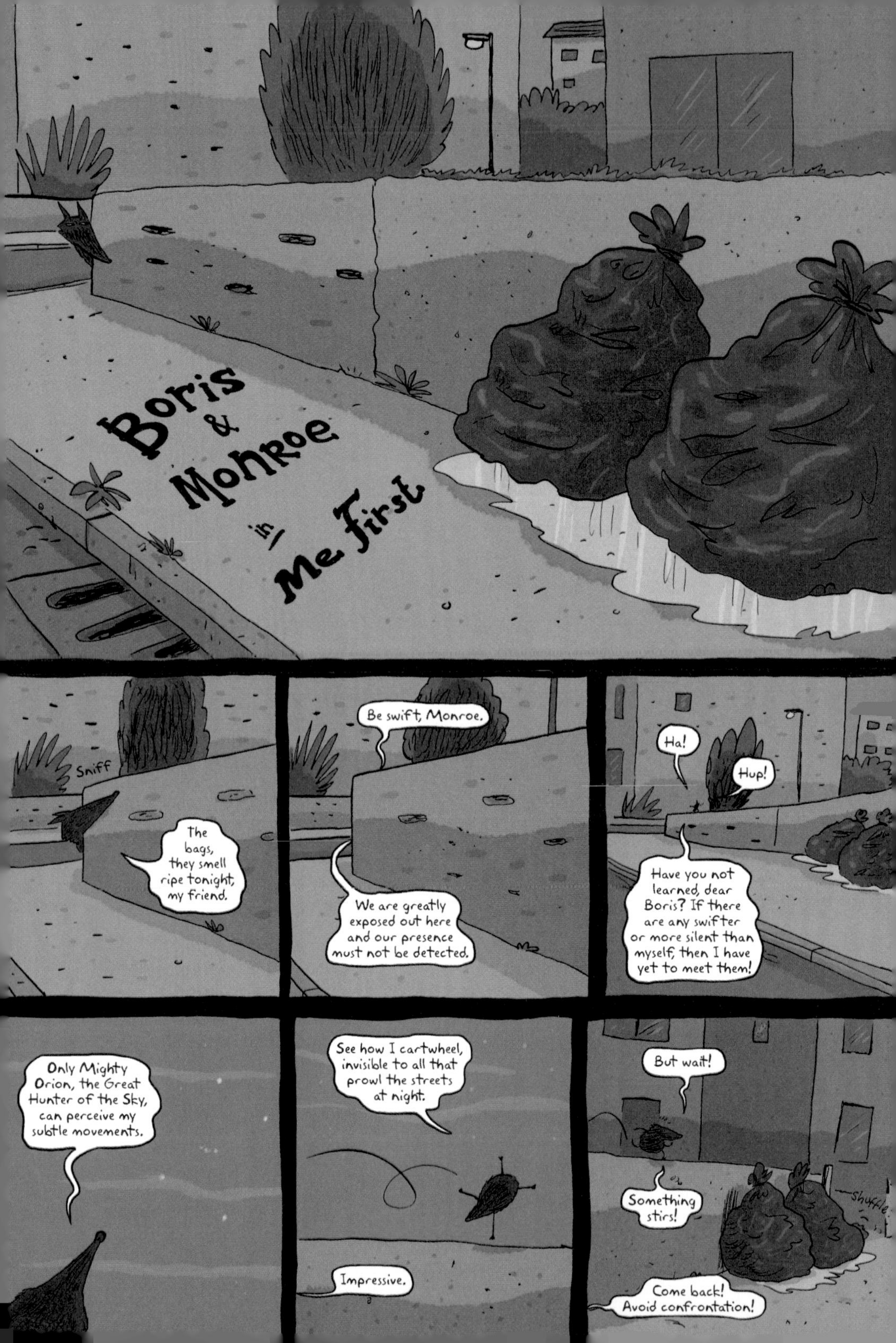
Boris & Monroe in Me First
Sniff
The bags, they smell ripe tonight, my friend.
Be swift, Monroe.
We are greatly exposed out here and our presence must not be detected.
Ha!
Hup!
Have you not learned, dear Boris? If there are any swifter or more silent than myself, then I have yet to meet them!
Only Mighty Orion, the Great Hunter of the Sky, can perceive my subtle movements.
See how I cartwheel, invisible to all that prowl the streets at night.
Impressive.
But wait!
Something stirs!
shuffle
Come back! Avoid confrontation!

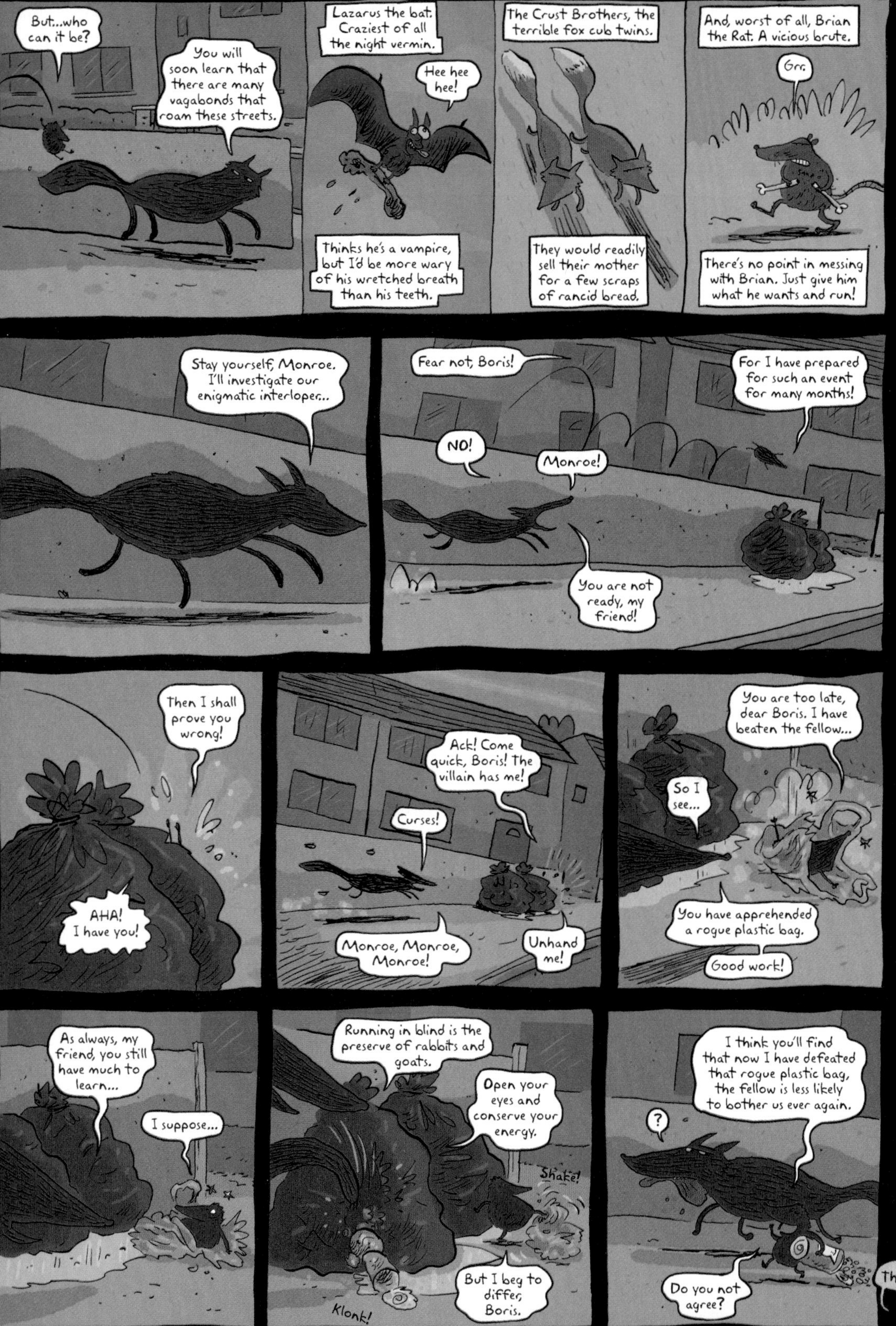
But...who can it be?
You will soon learn that there are many vagabonds that roam these streets.
Lazarus the bat. Craziest of all the night vermin.
Hee hee hee!
Thinks he's a vampire, but I'd be more wary of his wretched breath than his teeth.
The Crust Brothers, the terrible fox cub twins.
They would readily sell their mother for a few scraps of rancid bread.
And, worst of all, Brian the Rat. A vicious brute.
Grr.
There's no point in messing with Brian. Just give him what he wants and run!
Stay yourself, Monroe. I'll investigate our enigmatic interloper...
Fear not, Boris!
For I have prepared for such an event for many months!
NO!
Monroe!
You are not ready, my friend!
Then I shall prove you wrong!
AHA! I have you!
Ack! Come quick, Boris! The villain has me!
Curses!
Monroe, Monroe, Monroe!
Unhand me!
You are too late, dear Boris. I have beaten the fellow...
So I see...
You have apprehended a rogue plastic bag.
Good work!
As always, my friend, you still have much to learn...
I suppose...
Running in blind is the preserve of rabbits and goats.
Open your eyes and conserve your energy.
Shake!
But I beg to differ, Boris.
Klonk!
I think you'll find that now I have defeated that rogue plastic bag, the fellow is less likely to bother us ever again.
?
Do you not agree?
The End!

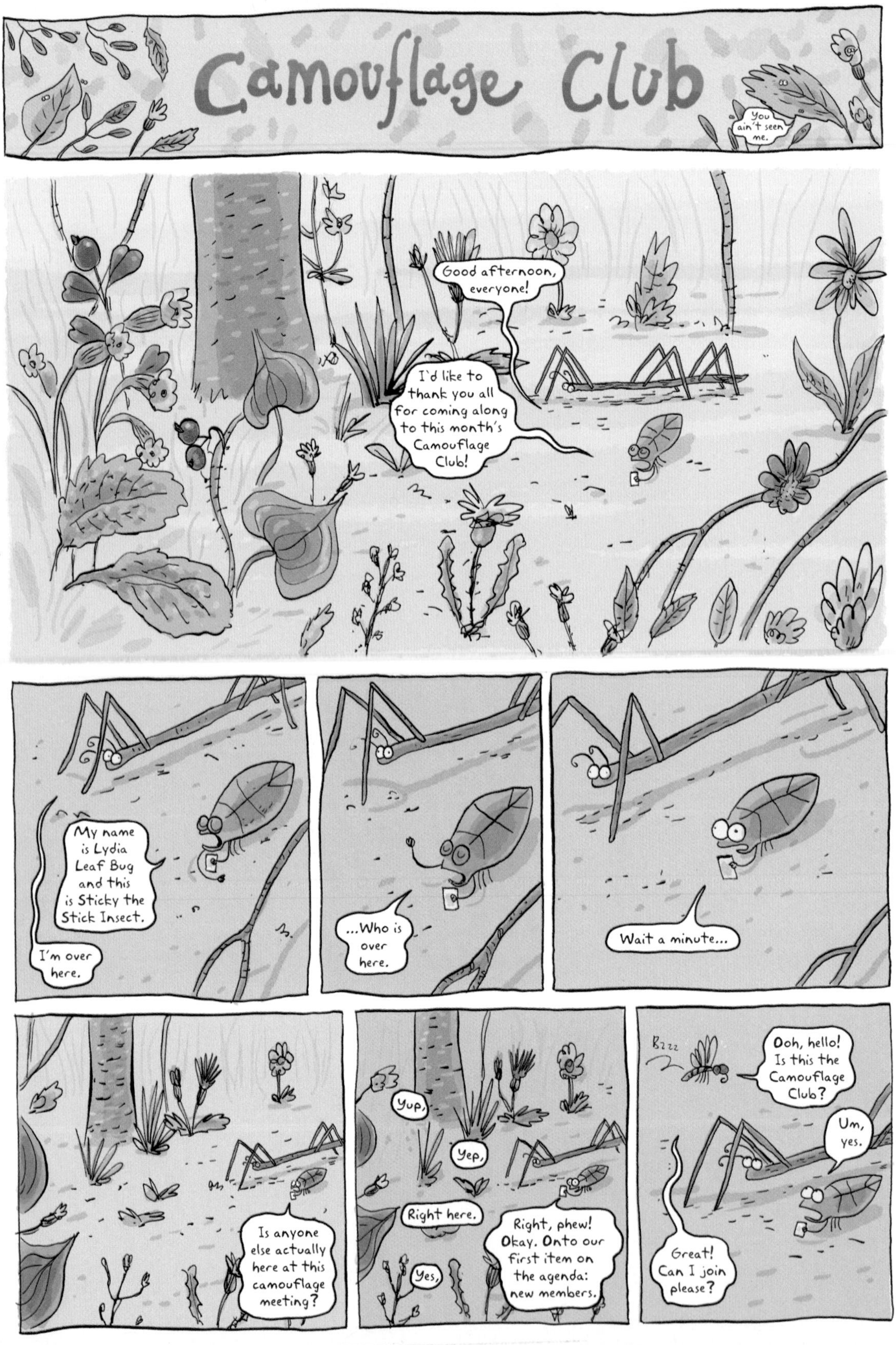

Camouflage Club
You ain't seen me.
Good afternoon, everyone!
I'd like to thank you all for coming along to this month's Camouflage Club!
My name is Lydia Leaf Bug and this is Sticky the Stick Insect.
I'm over here.
...Who is over here.
Wait a minute...
Is anyone else actually here at this camouflage meeting?
Yup,
Yep,
Right here.
Yes,
Right, phew! Okay. Onto our first item on the agenda: new members.
Bzzz
Ooh, hello! Is this the Camouflage Club?
Um, yes.
Great! Can I join please?

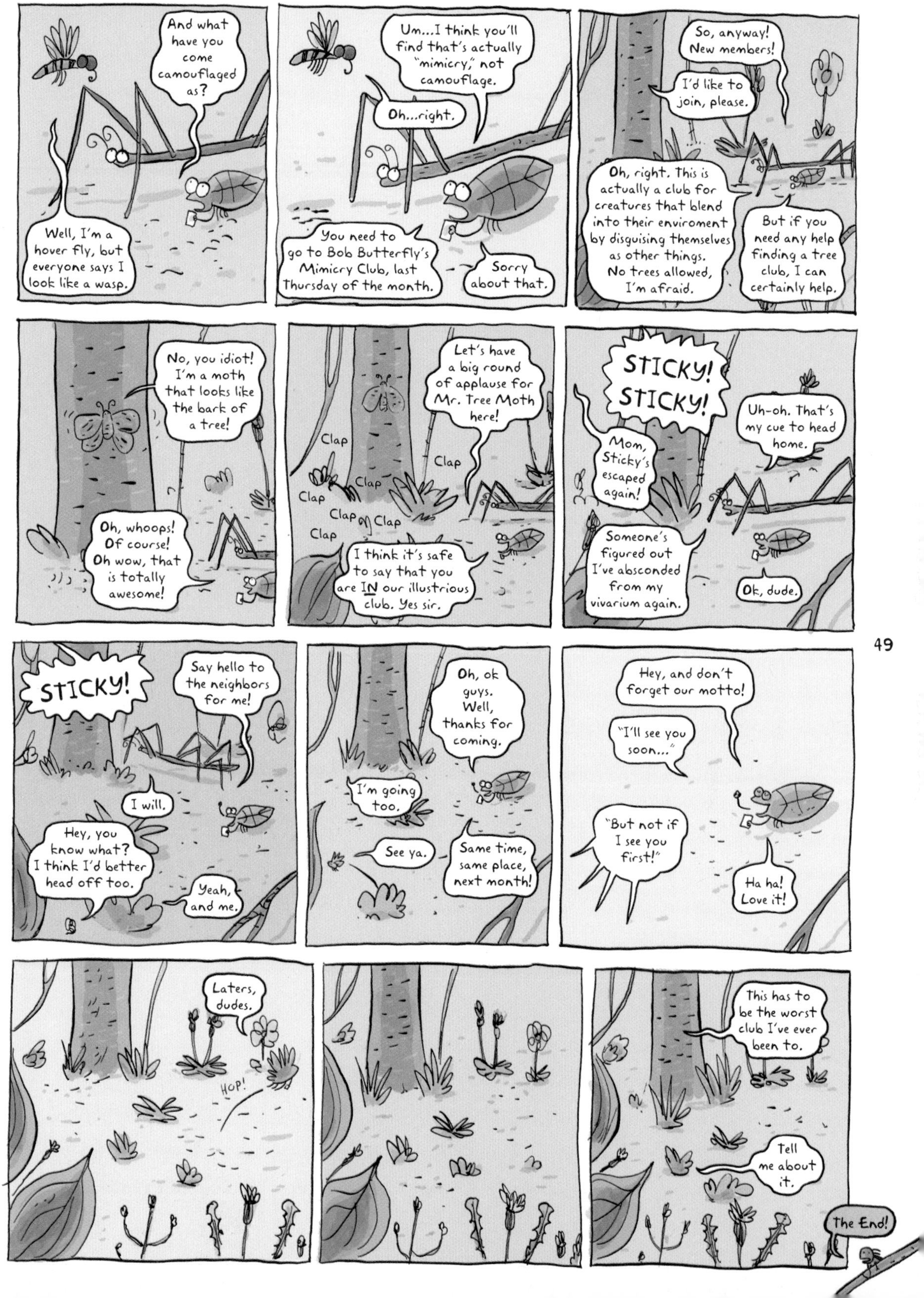
And what have you come camouflaged as?
Well, I'm a hover fly, but everyone says I look like a wasp.
Um...I think you'll find that's actually "mimicry," not camouflage.
Oh...right.
You need to go to Bob Butterfly's Mimicry Club, last Thursday of the month.
Sorry about that.
So, anyway! New members!
I'd like to join, please.
Oh, right. This is actually a club for creatures that blend into their enviroment by disguising themselves as other things. No trees allowed, I'm afraid.
But if you need any help finding a tree club, I can certainly help.
No, you idiot! I'm a moth that looks like the bark of a tree!
Oh, whoops! Of course! Oh wow, that is totally awesome!
Let's have a big round of applause for Mr. Tree Moth here!
Clap
Clap
Clap
Clap
Clap
Clap
Clap
I think it's safe to say that you are IN our illustrious club. Yes sir.
STICKY! STICKY!
Mom, Sticky's escaped again!
Uh-oh. That's my cue to head home.
Someone's figured out I've absconded from my vivarium again.
Ok, dude.
STICKY!
Say hello to the neighbors for me!
I will.
Hey, you know what? I think I'd better head off too.
Yeah, and me.
Oh, ok guys. Well, thanks for coming.
I'm going too.
See ya.
Same time, same place, next month!
Hey, and don't forget our motto!
"I'll see you soon..."
"But not if I see you first!"
Ha ha! Love it!
Laters, dudes.
HOP!
This has to be the worst club I've ever been to.
Tell me about it.
The End!

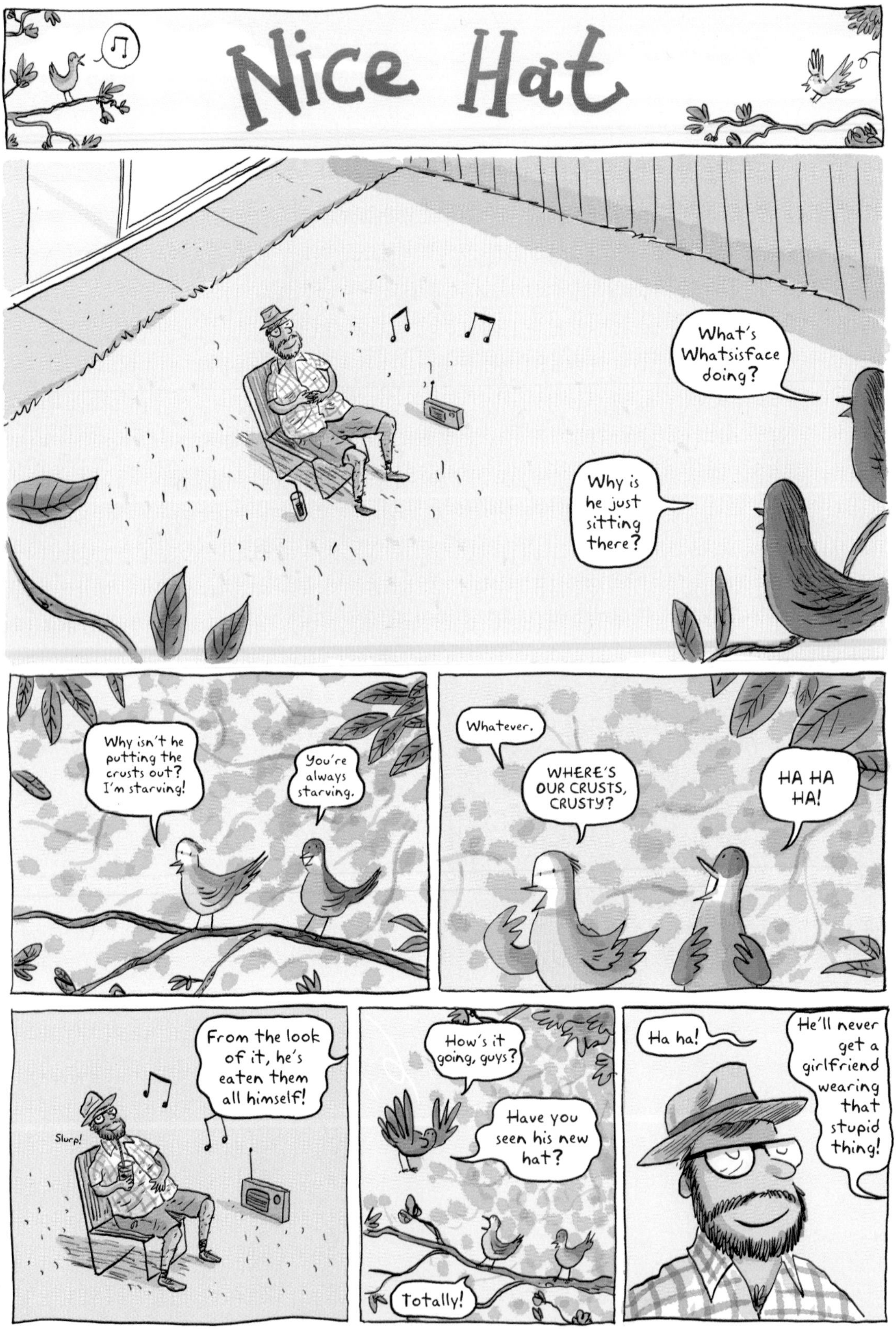
Nice Hat
What's Whatsisface doing?
Why is he just sitting there?
Why isn't he putting the crusts out? I'm starving!
You're always starving.
Whatever.
WHERE'S OUR CRUSTS, CRUSTY?
HA HA HA!
From the look of it, he's eaten them all himself!
Slurp!
How's it going, guys?
Have you seen his new hat?
Totally!
Ha ha!
He'll never get a girlfriend wearing that stupid thing!

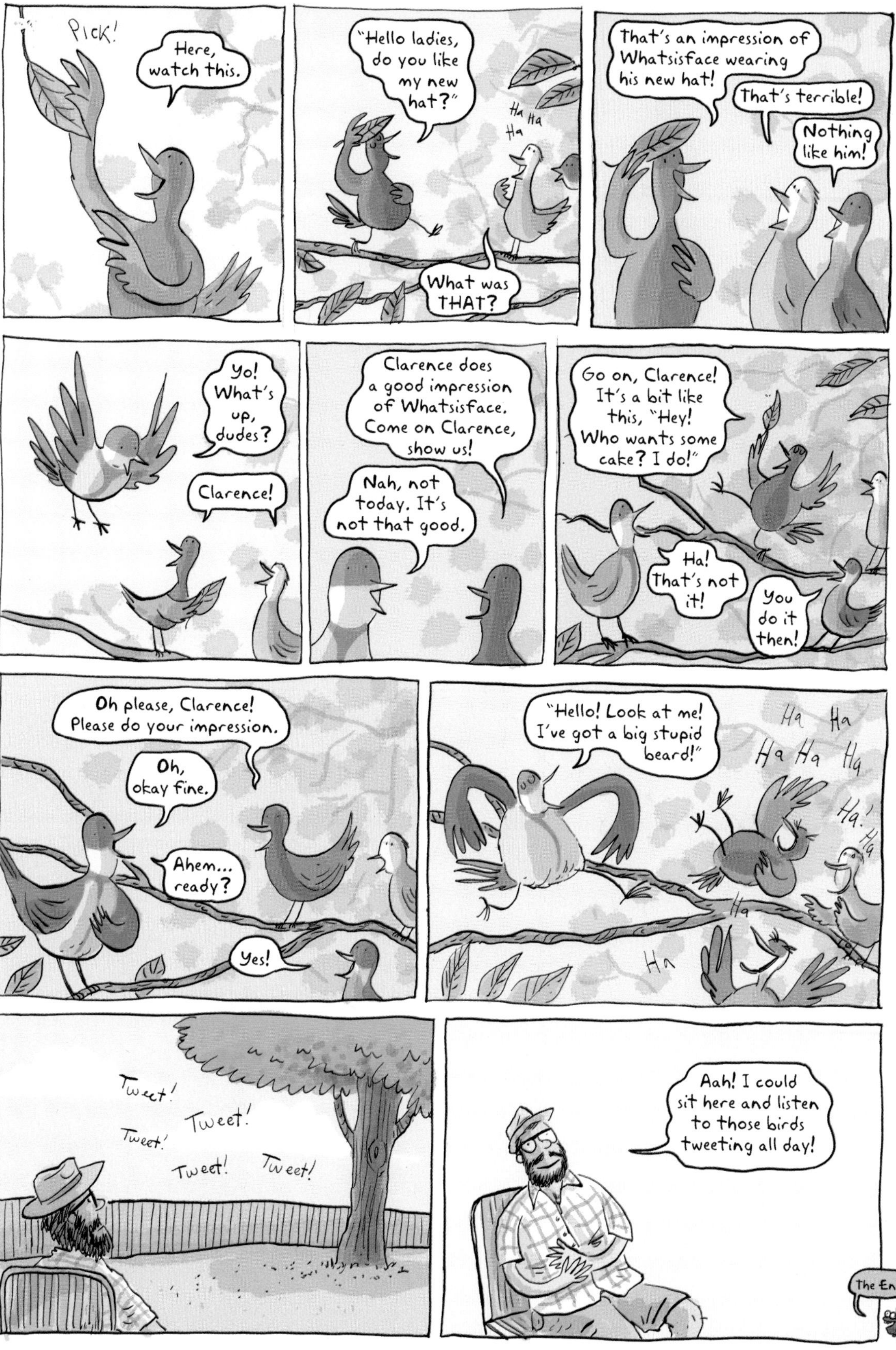
PICK!
Here, watch this.
"Hello ladies, do you like my new hat?"
Ha Ha Ha
What was THAT?
That's an impression of Whatsisface wearing his new hat!
That's terrible!
Nothing like him!
Yo! What's up, dudes?
Clarence!
Clarence does a good impression of Whatsisface. Come on Clarence, show us!
Nah, not today. It's not that good.
Go on, Clarence! It's a bit like this, "Hey! Who wants some cake? I do!"
Ha! That's not it!
You do it then!
Oh please, Clarence! Please do your impression.
Oh, okay fine.
Ahem... ready?
Yes!
"Hello! Look at me! I've got a big stupid beard!"
Ha Ha Ha Ha Ha Ha! Ha Ha Ha
Tweet! Tweet! Tweet! Tweet! Tweet!
Aah! I could sit here and listen to those birds tweeting all day!
The End!

Grumpy Spiders

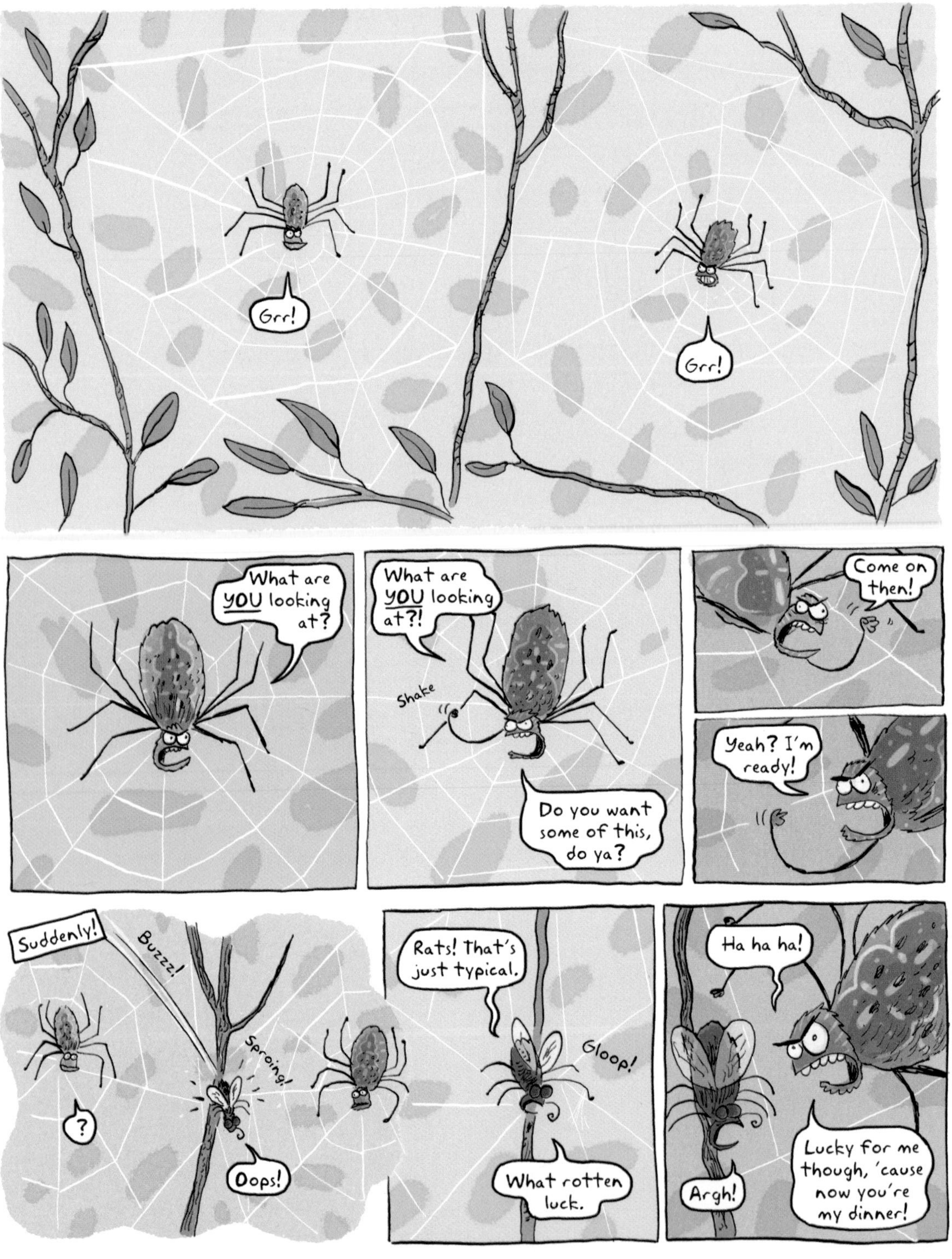

Grr!
Grr!
What are YOU looking at?
What are YOU looking at?!
Shake
Do you want some of this, do ya?
Come on then!
Yeah? I'm ready!
Suddenly!
Buzzz!
Sproing!
?
Oops!
Rats! That's just typical.
Gloop!
What rotten luck.
Ha ha ha!
Argh!
Lucky for me though, 'cause now you're my dinner!

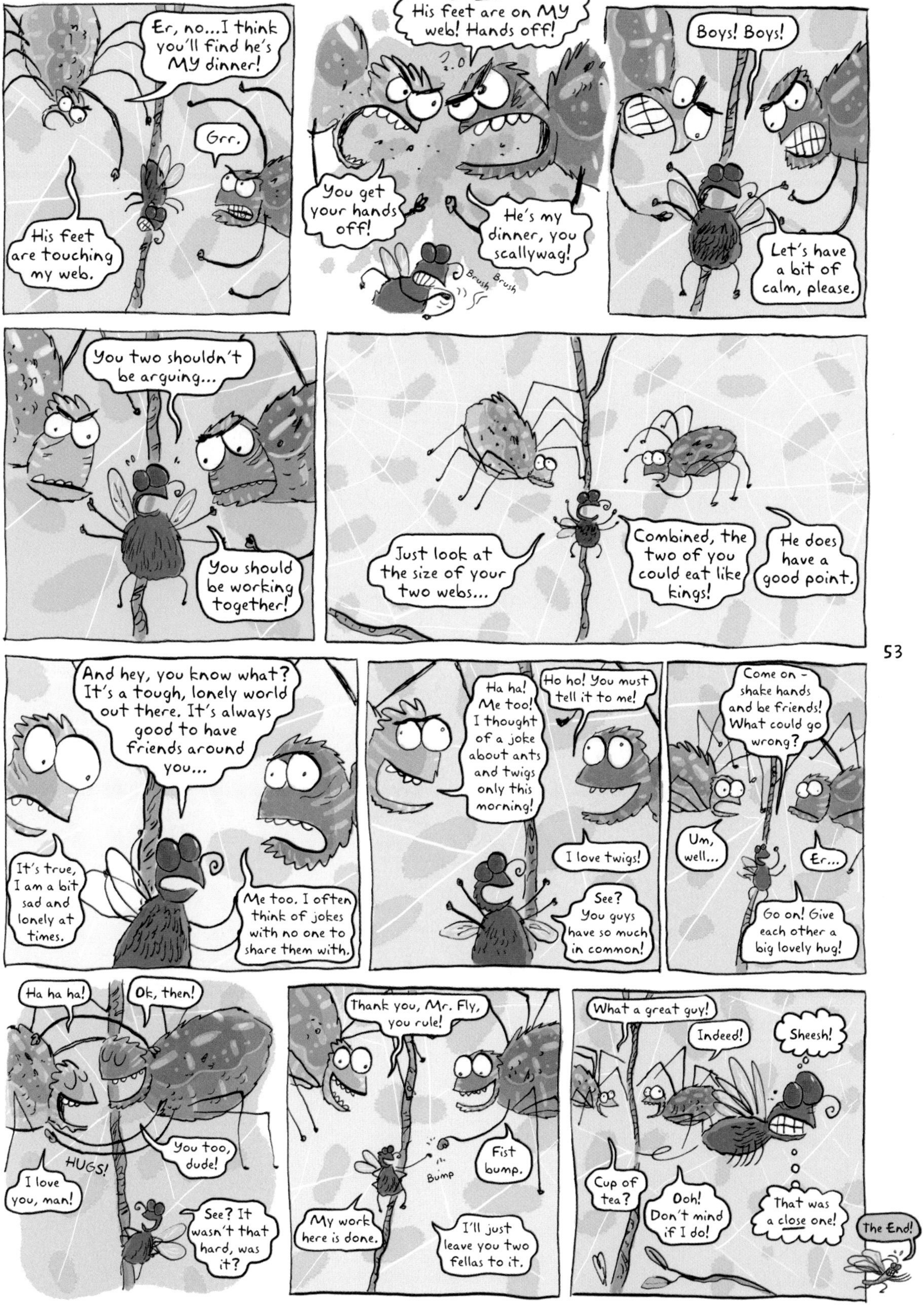
Er, no...I think you'll find he's MY dinner!
Grr.
His feet are touching my web.
His feet are on MY web! Hands off!
You get your hands off!
He's my dinner, you scallywag!
Brush Brush
Boys! Boys!
Let's have a bit of calm, please.
You two shouldn't be arguing...
You should be working together!
Just look at the size of your two webs...
Combined, the two of you could eat like kings!
He does have a good point.
And hey, you know what? It's a tough, lonely world out there. It's always good to have friends around you...
It's true, I am a bit sad and lonely at times.
Me too. I often think of jokes with no one to share them with.
Ha ha! Me too! I thought of a joke about ants and twigs only this morning!
Ho ho! You must tell it to me!
I love twigs!
See? You guys have so much in common!
Come on - shake hands and be friends! What could go wrong?
Um, well...
Er...
Go on! Give each other a big lovely hug!
Ha ha ha!
Ok, then!
HUGS!
I love you, man!
You too, dude!
See? It wasn't that hard, was it?
Thank you, Mr. Fly, you rule!
Fist bump.
Bump
My work here is done.
I'll just leave you two fellas to it.
What a great guy!
Indeed!
Sheesh!
Cup of tea?
Ooh! Don't mind if I do!
That was a close one!
The End!

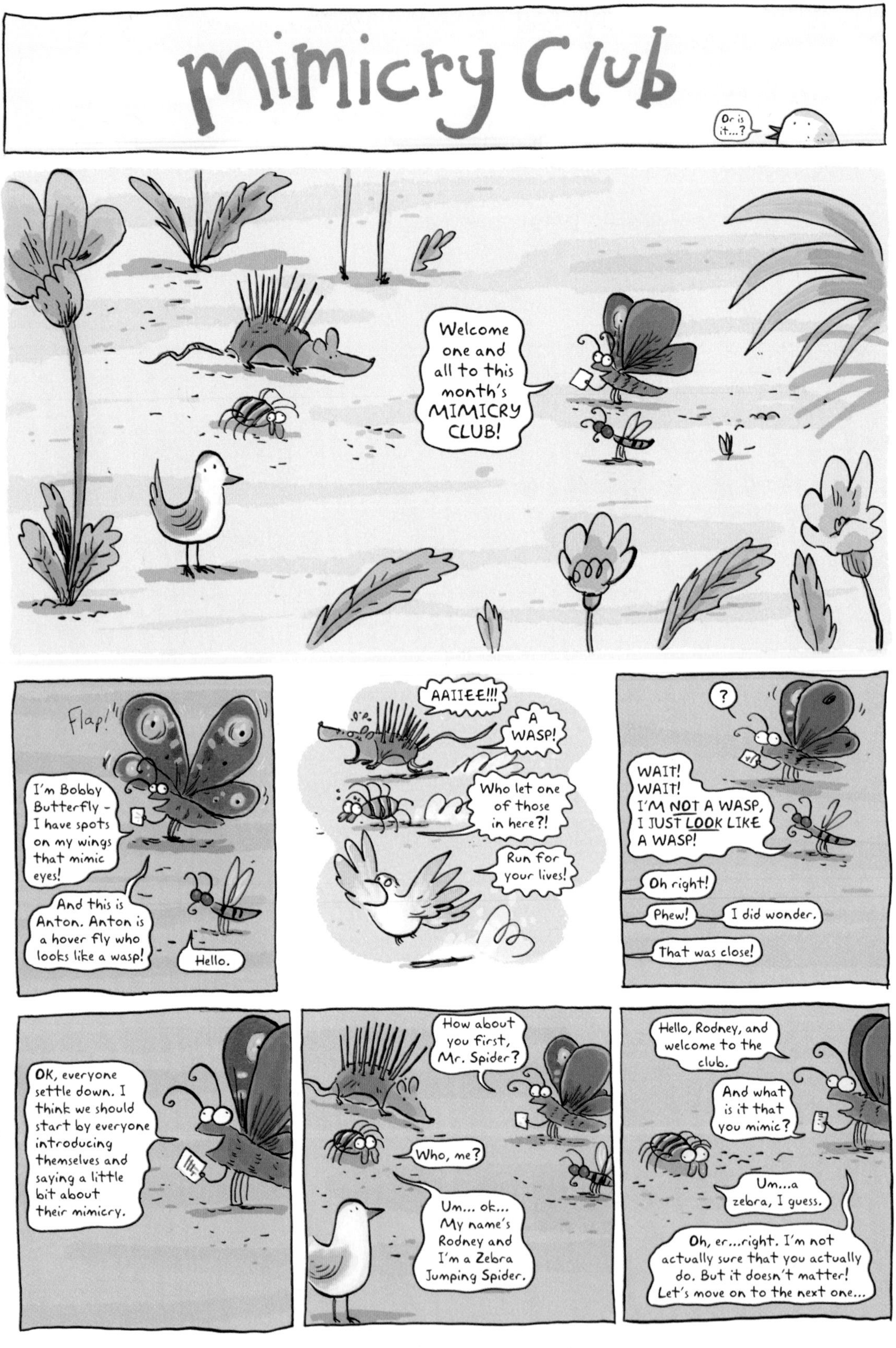
Mimicry Club
Or is it...?
Welcome one and all to this month's MIMICRY CLUB!
Flap!
I'm Bobby Butterfly - I have spots on my wings that mimic eyes!
And this is Anton. Anton is a hover fly who looks like a wasp!
Hello.
AAIIEE!!!
A WASP!
Who let one of those in here?!
Run for your lives!
?
WAIT! WAIT! I'M NOT A WASP, I JUST LOOK LIKE A WASP!
Oh right!
Phew!
I did wonder.
That was close!
OK, everyone settle down. I think we should start by everyone introducing themselves and saying a little bit about their mimicry.
How about you first, Mr. Spider?
Who, me?
Um... ok... My name's Rodney and I'm a Zebra Jumping Spider.
Hello, Rodney, and welcome to the club.
And what is it that you mimic?
Um...a zebra, I guess.
Oh, er...right. I'm not actually sure that you actually do. But it doesn't matter! Let's move on to the next one...

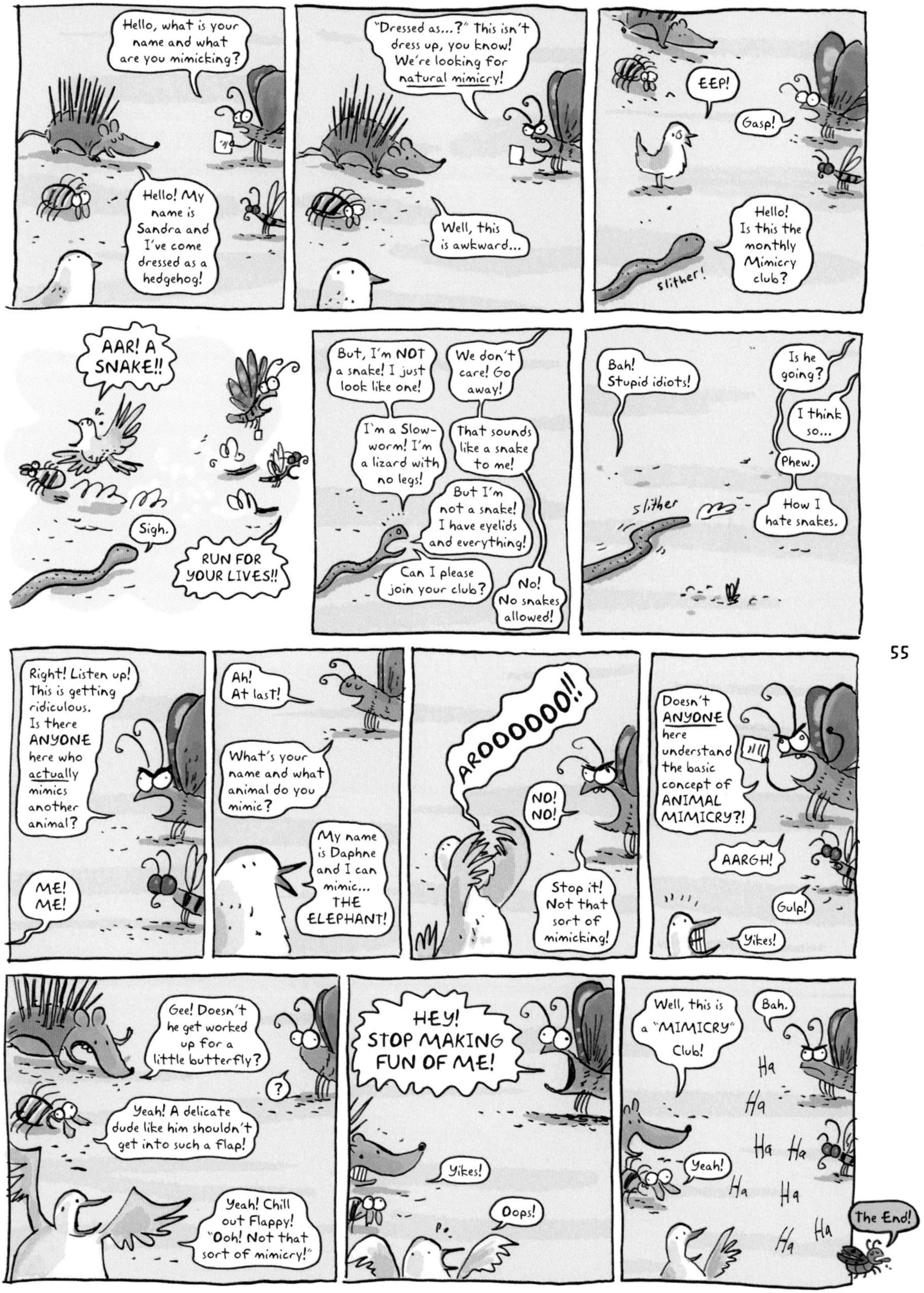

Hello, what is your name and what are you mimicking?
Hello! My name is Sandra and I've come dressed as a hedgehog!
"Dressed as...?" This isn't dress up, you know! We're looking for natural mimicry!
Well, this is awkward...
EEP!
Gasp!
Hello! Is this the monthly Mimicry club?
slither!
AAR! A SNAKE!!
Sigh.
RUN FOR YOUR LIVES!!
But, I'm NOT a snake! I just look like one!
We don't care! Go away!
I'm a Slow-worm! I'm a lizard with no legs!
That sounds like a snake to me!
But I'm not a snake! I have eyelids and everything!
Can I please join your club?
No! No snakes allowed!
Bah! Stupid idiots!
Is he going?
I think so...
Phew.
How I hate snakes.
slither
Right! Listen up! This is getting ridiculous. Is there ANYONE here who actually mimics another animal?
ME! ME!
Ah! At last!
What's your name and what animal do you mimic?
My name is Daphne and I can mimic... THE ELEPHANT!
AROOOOOO!!
NO! NO!
Stop it! Not that sort of mimicking!
Doesn't ANYONE here understand the basic concept of ANIMAL MIMICRY?!
AARGH!
Gulp!
Yikes!
Gee! Doesn't he get worked up for a little butterfly?
?
Yeah! A delicate dude like him shouldn't get into such a flap!
Yeah! Chill out Flappy! "Ooh! Not that sort of mimicry!"
HEY! STOP MAKING FUN OF ME!
Yikes!
Oops!
Well, this is a "MIMICRY" Club!
Bah.
Ha Ha Ha Ha Ha Ha Ha Ha
Yeah!
The End!

Mr. Leaf

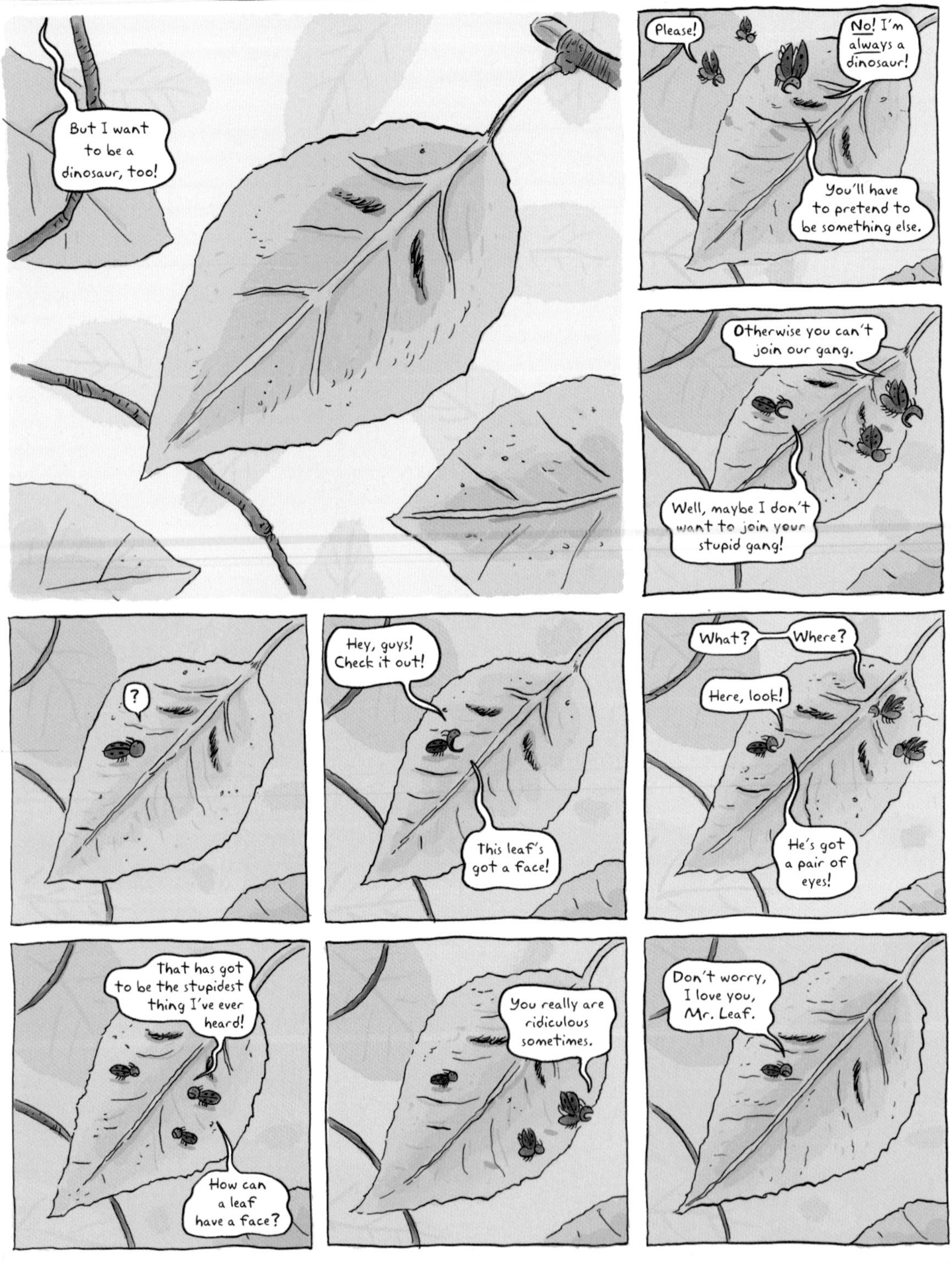

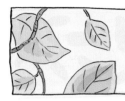

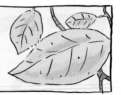

But I want to be a dinosaur, too!
Please!
No! I'm always a dinosaur!
You'll have to pretend to be something else.
Otherwise you can't join our gang.
Well, maybe I don't want to join your stupid gang!
?
Hey, guys! Check it out!
This leaf's got a face!
What?
Where?
Here, look!
He's got a pair of eyes!
That has got to be the stupidest thing I've ever heard!
How can a leaf have a face?
You really are ridiculous sometimes.
Don't worry, I love you, Mr. Leaf.

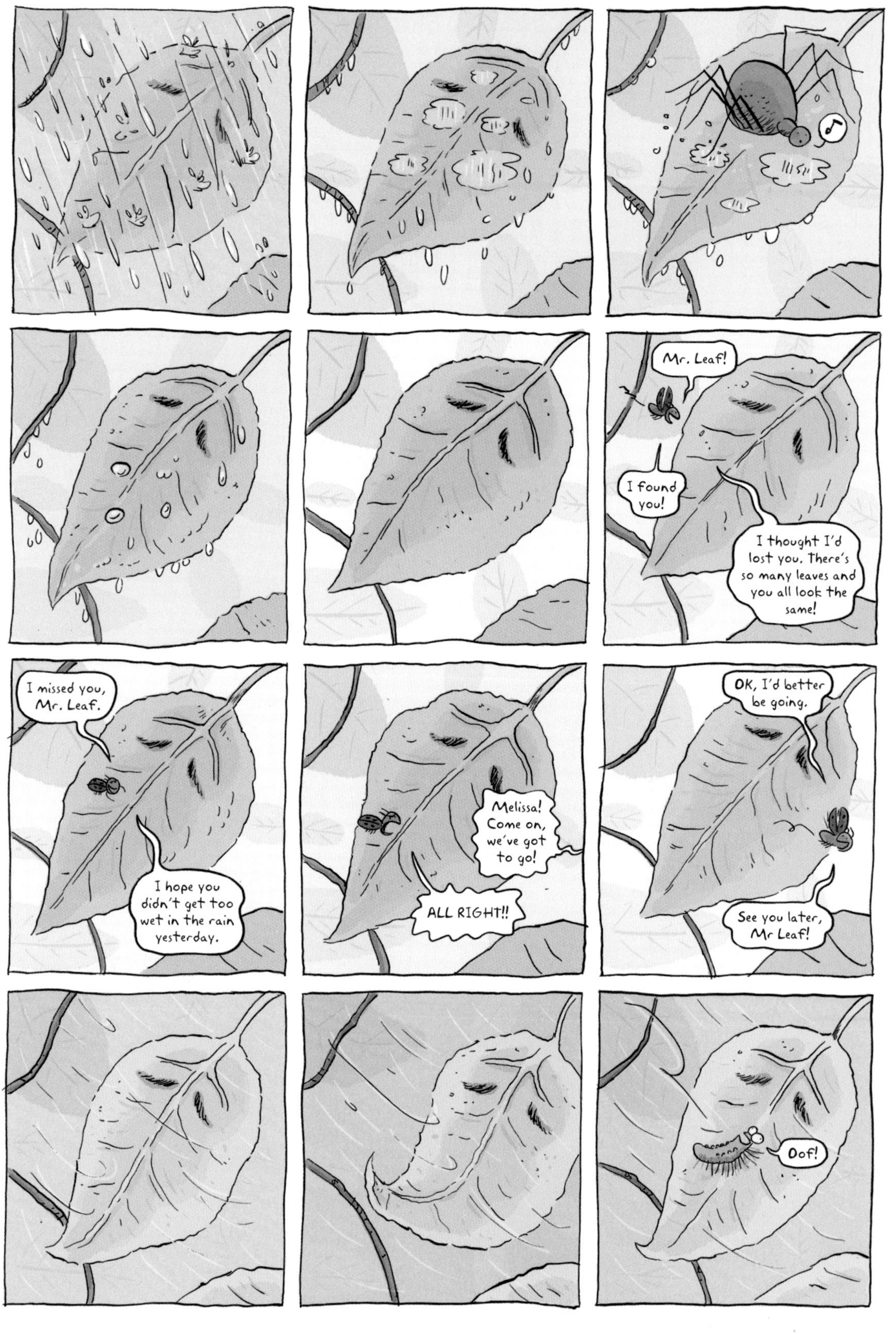
Mr. Leaf!
I found you!
I thought I'd lost you. There's so many leaves and you all look the same!
I missed you, Mr. Leaf.
I hope you didn't get too wet in the rain yesterday.
Melissa! Come on, we've got to go!
ALL RIGHT!!
OK, I'd better be going.
See you later, Mr Leaf!
Oof!

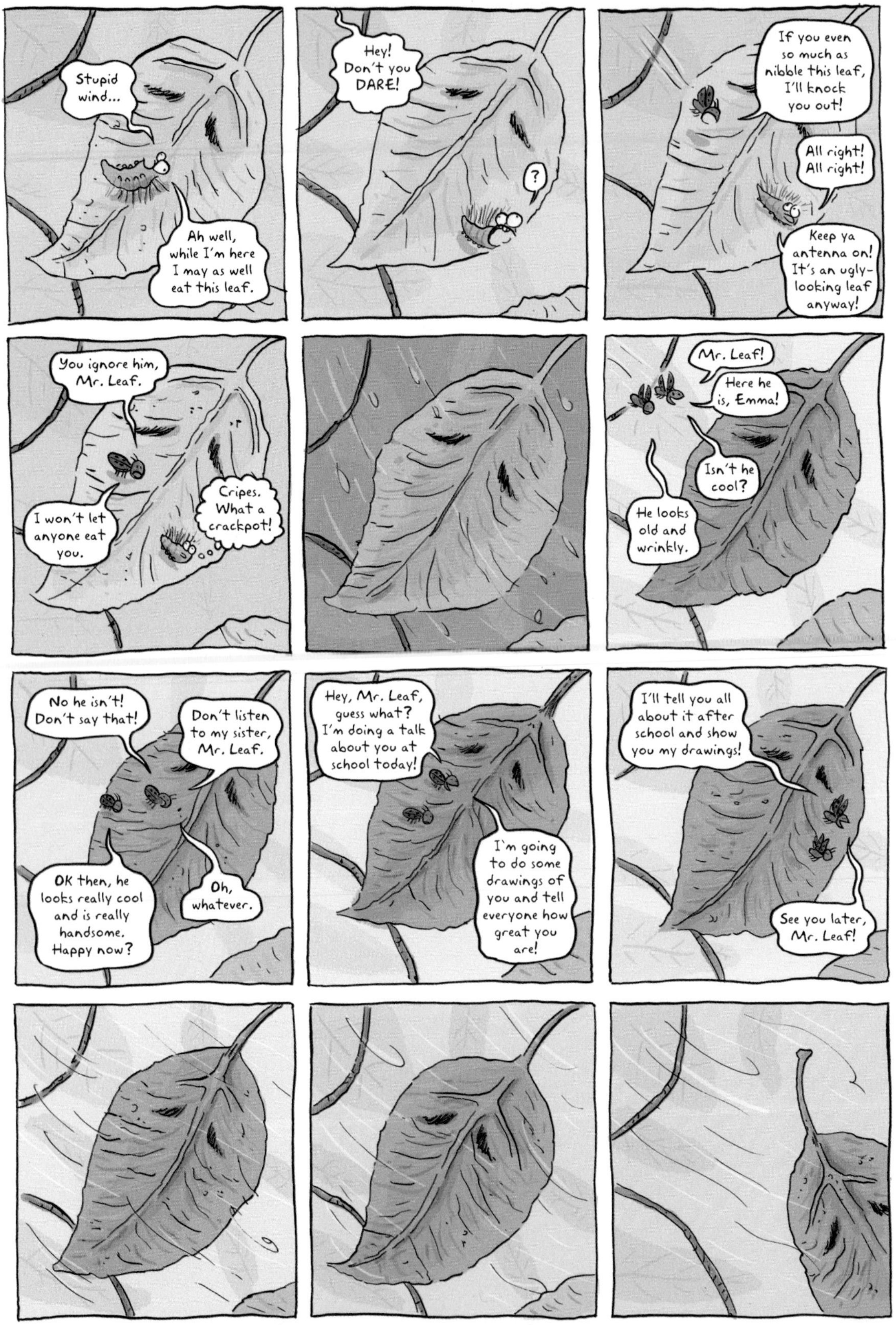
Stupid wind...
Ah well, while I'm here I may as well eat this leaf.
Hey! Don't you DARE!
?
If you even so much as nibble this leaf, I'll knock you out!
All right! All right!
Keep ya antenna on! It's an ugly-looking leaf anyway!
You ignore him, Mr. Leaf.
I won't let anyone eat you.
Cripes. What a crackpot!
Mr. Leaf!
Here he is, Emma!
Isn't he cool?
He looks old and wrinkly.
No he isn't! Don't say that!
Don't listen to my sister, Mr. Leaf.
OK then, he looks really cool and is really handsome. Happy now?
Oh, whatever.
Hey, Mr. Leaf, guess what? I'm doing a talk about you at school today!
I'm going to do some drawings of you and tell everyone how great you are!
I'll tell you all about it after school and show you my drawings!
See you later, Mr. Leaf!

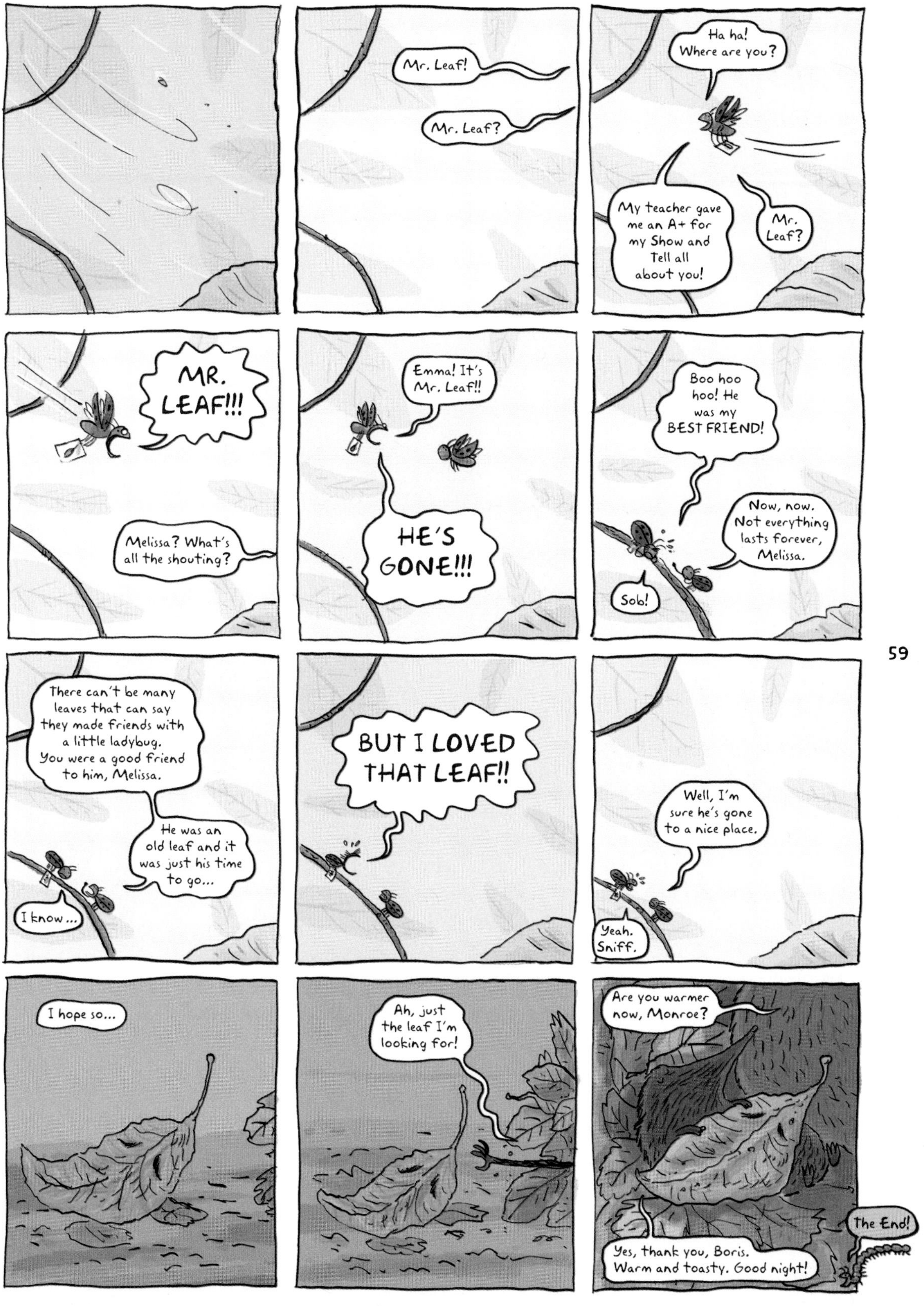
Mr. Leaf!
Mr. Leaf?
Ha ha! Where are you?
My teacher gave me an A+ for my Show and Tell all about you!
Mr. Leaf?
MR. LEAF!!!
Melissa? What's all the shouting?
Emma! It's Mr. Leaf!!
HE'S GONE!!!
Boo hoo hoo! He was my BEST FRIEND!
Sob!
Now, now. Not everything lasts forever, Melissa.
There can't be many leaves that can say they made friends with a little ladybug. You were a good friend to him, Melissa.
He was an old leaf and it was just his time to go...
I know...
BUT I LOVED THAT LEAF!!
Well, I'm sure he's gone to a nice place.
Yeah. Sniff.
I hope so...
Ah, just the leaf I'm looking for!
Are you warmer now, Monroe?
Yes, thank you, Boris. Warm and toasty. Good night!
The End!

Gary's Garden
TOP CHUMPS

WHO HAS THE MOST LEGS? WHO IS THE ICKIEST IN THE GARDEN?
WHO IS THE WORLD'S MOST ROTTEN AND WHO IS THE TOP CHUMP?
GET THE LOWDOWN ON YOUR GARY'S GARDEN FAVORITES WITH
THIS HANDY GUIDE!

CHOMPY

Intelligence	2
Heroism	4
Grumpiness	9
Ickiness	8
Legs	16

Grumpy caterpillar, forever annoying his butterfly brother, Bert. Quite enjoys rollicking adventures with mad ladybugs.

RUPERT

Intelligence	6
Heroism	5
Grumpiness	7
Ickiness	2
Legs	4

Skittish nutjob. Do NOT steal his acorns. Or even LOOK at his acorns. In fact forget I even mentioned his stupid acorns.

WIGGLES

Intelligence	2
Heroism	2
Grumpiness	1
Ickiness	10
Legs	0

The happiest caterpillar in the garden. Loves that her best friend is ANOTHER caterpillar. Yay! Wiggles and Chompy BFF!

JENNIFER

Intelligence	6
Heroism	3
Grumpiness	9
Ickiness	9
Legs	Just the 2

Should be a frog, but isn't a frog. Should have four legs, but only has two. Life was much more fun when no one had any legs.

DAPHNE

Intelligence	3
Heroism	7
Grumpiness	2
Ickiness	6
Legs	2

Loves twigs and art and can do a pretty mean elephant impression. Would join more clubs if only there were enough hours in the day.

MONROE

Intelligence	7
Heroism	10
Grumpiness	1
Ickiness	2
Legs	4

Apprentice nighttime ninja. Eager to please his master, Boris, and thinks he's ready to go it alone. Boris has different ideas...

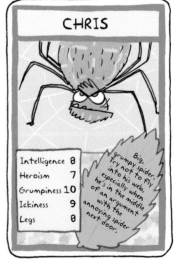

CHRIS

Intelligence	8
Heroism	7
Grumpiness	10
Ickiness	9
Legs	8

Big, grumpy spider. Try not to fly into his web, especially when he's in the middle of an argument with the annoying spider next door.

PROF. ZARPOV

Intelligence	10
Heroism	9
Grumpiness	4
Ickiness	7
Legs	6

At the forefront of ladybug science. Explorer of inter-dimensional worlds using hi-tech contraptions of his own invention.

LYDIA

Intelligence	8
Heroism	7
Grumpiness	1
Ickiness	9
Legs	6

Looking like a leaf is probably the greatest thing to happen to Lydia. Her best friend is a stick insect who looks like a twig! Would now like a friend who looks like a flower.

RONALD

Intelligence	9
Heroism	4
Grumpiness	1
Ickiness	9
Legs	8

Ronald loves to entertain and is always on the lookout for a captive audience for his brilliant new jokes and dance moves.

PENNY

Intelligence	6
Heroism	4
Grumpiness	4
Ickiness	7
Legs	2

Frequent visitor to the garden, but doesn't interact much with the others, especially as it diverts attention from any crusts that have to be eaten.

STICKY

Intelligence	9
Heroism	5
Grumpiness	1
Ickiness	10
Legs	6

Lives next door, but prefers the company of Gary's Garden. Although everyone gets on his nerves there too, to be frank.

BORIS

Intelligence	9
Heroism	10
Grumpiness	6
Ickiness	3
Legs	4

Expert nighttime ninja. Has taken promising hedgehog Monroe under his wing. Can barely handle his rudeness, let alone much else.

HARRIET

Intelligence	7
Heroism	7
Grumpiness	4
Ickiness	2
Legs	2

Sociable little bird who appreciates having a little gang to hang around with. Wishes there was more than just breadcrumbs to eat, though.

BRIAN

Intelligence	8
Heroism	1
Grumpiness	9
Ickiness	10
Legs	4

They don't come nastier, stinkier or er... rottener than nighttime villain Brian the rat. Really likes a bag of chips for dinner.

LARRY

Intelligence	5
Heroism	10
Grumpiness	3
Ickiness	7
Legs	6

Lord of the jungle! Few are those that match his courage and taste for adventure. Even understands a little of the Ancient Ladybug language.

TERRENCE

Intelligence	7
Heroism	8
Grumpiness	8
Ickiness	9
Legs	1

Terrence just wants to go on crazy adventures stealing food and disappearing off into strange distant lands. Why DOESN'T HIS MOM UNDERSTAND?!

CLARENCE

Intelligence	7
Heroism	9
Scarcity	3
Ickiness	2
Legs	2

Happy-go-lucky. Great bird. Loves noodles, big underwear, and can do an amazing impression of "Whatsisface".

GARY

Intelligence	10
Heroism	10
Grumpiness	10
Ickiness	10
Legs	10

Oblivious owner of the garden. Loves all the little birdies and creepy-crawlies, but is not certain if that love is returned. (It's not.)

SANDRA

Well, this is awkward.

Intelligence	7
Heroism	5
Grumpiness	3
Ickiness	6
Legs	4

Loves to dress up at every occasion. Past costumes include a hedgehog, a bag of chips, a rock, and Troy Trailblazer.

ANTON

Intelligence	6
Heroism	5
Grumpiness	7
Ickiness	8
Legs	6

Hover Fly Anton keeps being told he looks like a wasp. Wishes he just looked like a hover fly and everyone would shut up.

MR. LEAF

Intelligence	0
Heroism	0
Grumpiness	9
Ickiness	0
Legs	0

A leaf with a face on it. Looks very old and wise, but probably isn't. Now serves as a blanket for ninja hedgehog Monroe.

BOBBY

Intelligence	7
Heroism	5
Grumpiness	8
Ickiness	3
Legs	6

Butterfly with impressive eyes on his wings. Not that he can see with them or anything. Don't mention Camouflage Club.

JOHN

Intelligence	8
Heroism	10
Grumpiness	4
Ickiness	6
Legs	6

Inter-dimensional traveler. Has visited Mars, Zarpovia, and the distant future. Is very excited about his upcoming staycation.

BENNY

Intelligence	7
Heroism	3
Grumpiness	8
Ickiness	10
Legs	0

Weird being from Zarpovia, a new universe within a universe inside Gary's house. Chompy thinks it's a guppy, but what does he know?

TRISH

Intelligence	8
Heroism	4
Grumpiness	10
Ickiness	10
Legs	0

Little apple worm, suffering the problems of affordable housing, i.e. LOTS OF STUPID NOISY NEIGHBORS!!!

SHUT UP!

RODNEY

Intelligence	7
Heroism	3
Grumpiness	6
Ickiness	5
Legs	8

A lover of art, Rodney would one day love to be a famous artist. Or, if that doesn't work out, a zebra impersonator.

BERT

Intelligence	7
Heroism	8
Grumpiness	9
Ickiness	3
Legs	6

Chompy's grumpy brother Bert. Is grumpy because Chompy is such a fulltime idiot. How he wishes for a quiet life...

HENRY

Intelligence	8
Heroism	7
Grumpiness	3
Ickiness	6
Legs	8

Henry is very old and has seen many changes to the garden over the years. Wishes the youngsters would slow down a bit just for a chat!

GWENDOLIN

Intelligence	8
Heroism	6
Grumpiness	1
Ickiness	2
Legs	6

It's not often you get rescued by a dashing hero in a loincloth, but who was he? Where did he come from? And does he want his loincloth back?

RAY

Intelligence	7
Heroism	5
Grumpiness	7
Ickiness	9
Legs	0

Ray isn't a snake - he's not even a worm. He's a SLOWWORM, lizards without legs, just so you know. Not that anyone listens.

THELMA

Intelligence	9
Heroism	7
Grumpiness	1
Ickiness	4
Legs	4

Thelma has a good nose for food, so long as it's vegetarian. She does like worms, it's just that she couldn't eat a whole one.

HUMPHREY

Intelligence	8
Heroism	9
Grumpiness	2
Ickiness	9
Legs	6

Being a blue bottle means having your wits about you at all times. Fortunately, spiders are a bit stupid, so most nasty encounters are easily avoided. Barely.

MELISSA

Intelligence	8
Heroism	8
Grumpiness	4
Ickiness	3
Legs	6

Her best friend is Mr. Leaf. He's the only one who listens to Melissa and her troubles. She hopes Mr. Leaf appreciates the drawing she did of him!

GARY NORTHFIELD draws comic strips for several publications, including National Geographic Kids and The Phoenix. He is also the writer and illustrator of The Terrible Tales of the Teenytinysaurs! and Julius Zebra: Rumble with the Romans! Gary's Garden is his David Fickling Books/Scholastic debut. Gary lives in the United Kingdom. You can visit him online at www.garynorthfield.com.